Ink Monkey Press
Ink Monkey Press
Ink Monkey Press
Ink Monkey Press
Ink Monkey Press
Ink Monkey Press
Ink Monkey Press
Ink Monkey Press
Ink Monkey Press
Ink Monkey Press
Ink Monkey Press
Ink Monkey Press
Ink Monkey Press
Ink Monkey Press
Ink Monkey Press

Ink Monkey Press

You Don't Say

You Don't Say:
Stories in the Second-Person

Mandi M. Lynch
Editor

Catherine Gracey
Assistant Editor

Mandi M. Lynch would like to thank:

H. David Blalock for picking a title worth putting on the cover of an anthology & Mike Falcione for arguing the grammar/punctuation of the subtitle that I added...

the many authors who put their words on paper to make this happen & those who tried to help but couldn't...

Catherine Gracey, who agreed to the co-editor position without knowing what she was getting into...

The Incredible Stephen Zimmer, who answered questions and helped with things...

and her grandmother, who would have said "Oh, Honey, that's wonderful," had she been here to read this.

Catherine Gracey would like to thank:

Mandi and Lisa for their hospitality while she was in Nashville discussing this project.

Her family for being so understanding of time zone differences and sudden absences.

And most importantly the authors, both included and excluded from the finished anthology. ."Regardless of our decision to include a piece, I always learn something more about the craft with each reading."

You know what I'm talking about, even if you don't want to admit it. Second person. Inevitably, at some point around, oh, third grade, somebody raised their hand and asked your teacher why first and third existed but second didn't. Depending on the teacher, you were either told that it didn't exist or that it was out there, but then told not to use it. Ever.

Well, your teacher wasn't perfect. You know as well as anyone else that you can absolutely have a great story with second person as an important plot element. By starting with "you" as the subject, you are allowing the reader an extra-special bird's eye view of the story – from inside it as a character. It's a powerful device, and you're lucky to know it. What it isn't is terrible, horrible... abhorrant.

In these pages, you will be exposed to a select handful of authors who have mastered the fine art of "you." Authors who want you to live the story, feel every twist and turn that the main character feels. And right now, you're strapping yourself in and getting ready to go. After all, they're your stories, so you're in control.

What you won't find is anything that sounds like a choose-your-own-adventure story or a Dungeons and Dragons guide – those have been done to death. The point of this anthology is to demonstrate that maybe, just maybe, an incredible, mainstream story can come out of this as well; you know that better than most.

So sit back, get comfy, and turn the page. You're about to set off for the time of your life...

LIST OF STORIES

You turn the page, and begin to read...

Hunting the Hunter

A.M. Burns

The call came hours ago. It gave you time to head out. You didn't recognize the voice on the phone, but the instinct that runs so much of your life told you to trust it. Your full moon dinner sits untouched, now forgotten, as you stop the car along side the forest road.

Far to the east, the moon begins its rise. Even though the sun still hangs low on the western horizon, your heart races.

You move away from the car. An innocent may come by. You can't risk anyone else. There's already too much at stake.

The moon is close enough that you become part of the surrounding forest with ease, blending into the trees and rocks like the wolf within you. The wind carries a familiar scent. You acknowledge the truth of the warning as you start running, following the scent.

After a mile of rough terrain, feeling the moon grow ever closer in your blood, the pain hits you. You double over in mid stride, striking your knees hard on sharp rocks. This pain is nothing compared to the agony that rips through you as your body succumbs to the power of the full moon now glowing bright amongst the clouds above you.

The earth is soft and welcoming as your fingers thicken, flatten, becoming heavily-furred paws. Your back arches as shoulders and hips realign to allow greater movement in a four-legged form. When your head totally reshapes the worst pain strikes. Gone are the soft curves of your human face, replaced by the stark angles of the wolf's snout.

Your howl shatters the stillness of the twilight. Through amber eyes, the darkening forest is now almost noon bright.

With a final shake, the pain vanishes.

Your mind fights the instincts of the wolf. It's time to hunt, time to howl, time to run free, but you know there's something more important tonight. Through the wolf's keen nose, a familiar scent is strong.

Deep inside, the wolf realizes your mate is in danger. The need to protect the mate overpowers the instinct to hunt.

High steep paths are no longer an obstacle. Trails invisible to human eyes open up in light of the moon. Distances dissolve under the rush of paws, covering the ground in a rush of adrenaline and need.

Somewhere in the night an owl hoots before launching itself into the night. You listen to the silent wings as they cut through the still air. A whine escapes your lips. You want to hunt like the owl, but this is more important. Fail here and your mate dies. That part of you that is still human can not imagine life without Sam, the light of your life. Sam, who accepts what you are and still loves you.

You slow your rush. Sam's scent is stronger. You know he's near. If Sam's near the hunter is too. The need to rush in nearly over comes the knowledge that this is a trap, and you should proceed cautiously. You silence the growl that tries to escape through gritted teeth.

You walk around the small clearing, careful of where each paw lands, to avoid inadvertently snapping a trig, or crackling last year's leaves, possibly alerting the hunter of your arrival.

Keen eyes alert you to a small red beam crossing your path. Your human eyes would've missed the laser setting close to the ground. A quick glance shows little mirrors reflecting the beam around the small clearing.

Using the nature's stealth, you circle the clearing. Sam's normal musky scent is mingled with that of fear. That smell triggers conflicting emotions. The wolf now wonders if Sam is weak. Weak means prey. You push the instincts away with the need to protect Sam, weak or not. Whoever has scared Sam must pay for what they've done.

Mingled with the natural smells of the forest, you catch a whiff of deer musk.

It's the middle of summer. The deer won't be rutting for several more months.

Following the deer scent trail, the wind blows against your tail. You want to circle around. Approach from downwind. But you know there's no time. Find the deer scent and you find the hunter.

Just over a hundred yards from the clearing, there's a whiff of gun oil. It mingles with the smell of deer.

You glance around and spot a shadow clinging easily to the side of a tree. From the profile, the hunter's focused on the clearing.

Your paws aren't made for climbing. You know that you'd have no chance to climb the tree without the hunter bringing the gun down toward you.

Selecting a spot a couple of trees over from the hunter, close enough you can keep your keen senses alert, you settle down to wait. The wolf understands waiting to ambush prey.

The night draws on, every so often you hear Sam's familiar snores as the fear and exhaustion momentarily overcome him and he nods off. The comforting sounds makes you want to go and curl up around him.

At every movement, no matter how slight, you check to see if the hunter has started down the tree. So far it has only been seat shifting from time to time.

Finally with the night more than half gone, the hunter moves, the sound of bark breaking brings your head off your paws and you stare upward.

"Damn. Maybe I'll have better luck tomorrow night in town," a soft female voice says as the shadow starts down the trunk of the tree.

You rise silently to your feet. Long powerful claws dig angrily into the soft turf under them. All of your attention stays on the shadowy figure.

She slides gracefully down the narrow rope tied to the branch she'd perched upon. Her feet land almost wolf silent on the ground. With a deft flick of her wrist she loosens the rope from the branch and then catches the coils in her hand.

A mixed feeling of awe and fear stirs within you. She's obviously a skilled huntress. You wonder if you can take her in a fight, fair or otherwise.

With the rifle slung back over her shoulder she begins to stride toward the clearing where Sam waits.

This time you can't stop the growl that breaks the quiet night.

The hunter spins around toward you, but you're already in motion. You cover the space between the two of you in three massive leaps, the final one binging you down across her. The rifle goes flying before she can complete the easy motion of bringing it up to her shoulder.

As she goes down under you, she rolls to the side. Your claws rake across her as she rolls away.

She screams.

Her blood smells sweet on the night breeze.

You lunge after her. Your grasping teeth find her leg.

She screams again.

You smell the silver before you see the knife she brings up between you.

Instinct shouts at you to run from the knife. But she's threatened Sam. You must defend Sam.

The knife flashes down toward your muzzle, now wet with her blood. You let go of the leg, backing up for a better attack against the silver in her hand. The attack must be sure. The attack must be swift.

"Damn you!" she screams.

Your defiant howl splits the night. Your growl freezes her in place as your amber glare locks onto her delicate blue eyes. Holding her gaze, you will know before she makes a lunge with the silver knife. Humans always give themselves away with their eyes. She looks away a split second before she lunges toward you.

A cub could've dodged her attack. Your fangs close over the tiny bones in her wrist. With but the slightest pressure, you render the bones asunder.

The knife hits the ground before her screams end. Her hot sweet blood fills your mouth as you yank the arm away from the hunter.

She collapses on the ground, blood gushing out of the shattered stump of her shoulder. The ground beneath her quickly becomes saturated. You know she has no hope of surviving such a wound. You know that you haven't passed on the curse to another. Your howl of triumph rings through the forest.

"Honey? Is that you out there?" Sam's voice is little more than a whisper from the clearing.

Your need to make sure he's okay overrides the fear of him seeing you covered in an opponent's blood. You turn and walk into the clearing.

In the center of the clearing, Sam lies bound. You realize this is why you could not see him before, only smell him. He's on his side, with his back to you. You walk up, careful not to growl and scare him.

He jumps as you push your cold nose against his hand just below the hunter's skillful knots. His hand smells of comfort, peace, and home. The nylon ropes resist your teeth at first as you carefully pull and tear at them.

"Please be careful," Sam whispers, more to himself than you.

You'd never be able to forgive yourself if you inadvertently gave Sam the curse. You pull enough at the ropes, that Sam is able to pull his hands out.

Rolling over, he pulls the cloth from his head. His soft brown eyes meet your amber ones. The light of the setting moon is just enough that he can make out who you are. His dazzling smile erases the fear from his face. He throws his arms around your neck, heedless of the blood beginning to mat in your grey fur. "I knew you would find me." His voice comes in a hoarse choke. "That woman told me you were in danger, then when we got out here, you weren't here. She clubbed me, when I woke up she'd tied me up and left me as bait."

His cheek is soft under your tongue as you wish you could tell him it was going to be fine, that the hunter lay dead just outside the clearing.

The moon is beginning to set beyond the mountains. The fire in your blood dies back. Suddenly all the energy of the wolf begins to fade. You're tired. A whine escapes your lips as your legs collapse beneath you.

"Are you okay? Did she hurt you?" You feel Sam's arms around you as the wolf recedes for another month. You drift into sleep knowing that he will be at your side when the sun rises.

Slip

Amy Yolanda Castillo

It's been almost ten years since you did it.

There are brilliant people in the world—astronomers and physicists and people with knowledge so advanced that there isn't even a *title* for what they do—astonishing people who understand that time is a dimension, a quantifiable force in the universe, like velocity and wave energy.

But for your purposes, time doesn't matter. You know that it's only a construct, made by and for finite beings. Months, days, years, what are they but a way of measuring yourself against the inevitable? Time is meaningless because time is death. All those little colored coins you've carried around in your pockets and your purses, the ones they gave you after thirty days, and ninety days, and a year, and five years, the ones you accepted so graciously while everyone else applauded—what are they but tiny hunks of metal? What meaning can they have for you, if time is but an artifice?

Thinking this way makes it easier to negotiate with yourself at the preliminary stages, when you're still only *considering* whether to do it. And you *do* think about it, for a long time. Because you can't just *snatch* at it, not after so many years. You can't just walk into a bar and order a drink. It's not that easy. You have to be like Jacob, wrestling with a fiercely stubborn angel. You must measure all you have and all you've lost against every last one of your hopes and dreams.

But no, you will not wrestle. Instead, you will dance—tender, close, cheek to cheek with your lesser demons.

Some say there's no dance at all, just a series of warning signs. They are right, of course, but you will ignore them. You will dance and dance, dance the days and the nights away, before you let yourself be led back to the punch bowl.

Here is the waltz. You're angry all the time. You've slammed your fist down on the horn of your car so many times that it warbles and whimpers instead of producing a long, decisive *honk* when you're stuck in traffic, trying to send a message to all those assholes pulling out in front of you, the ones who keep forgetting to signal, who roll through stop signs. The ones who go too fast or too slow. You don't care about these people. They aren't people to you at all. Better that they should *die* than get in your way.

Here is the rhumba. You've managed to wear away the enamel on your molars, grinding your teeth, biting down every time you think you might say something horribly offensive, something that might cost you your job or your relationship or your friend. Now your teeth sting when you sip hot soup, or when you lap at a icy popsicle.

Here is the tango. Even though pills have never been your thing, you start taking the painkillers you stashed away a year ago, when you had surgery and the orthopedic surgeon offered to prescribe Vicodin for the pain, but you lied and asked him to give you Percocet instead, not because it makes you hurt less, but because you get a lot more buzzed on oxy and it just feels good, *safe*, to know those pills are stashed away, in case you need them. Which you did.

But are those omens? Do they augur the end of all good things?

If you said yes, if you admitted it to be true, you would not give in. You would address your problems, your cravings, your *feelings* squarely. But truth be told, that's not really what you want. You're tired of all that. It's hard. So you deny that there are any warning signs. Because you are delusional, you say they are just promises of good things to come. Good times, good times.

When there have been enough promises, enough agonizing and soul-searching about whether you should do it, you give in. You are coming out of your skin, and there is only one thing that will afford relief. What sense is there in suffering needlessly?

You always said that if you went back, you'd buy a bottle of the top shelf liquor, the kind you used to buy way back when, around the time that everything went to hell and you didn't care anymore about the balance in your checking account, and you collected overdraft slips like playing cards in a game of Go Fish.

But that isn't what you wind up doing. You know that what you are doing is right, but you also know that it is wrong. So you go to Hogan's, which is the shadiest liquor store in your neighborhood. You look for the whiskey, for your brand, and you blanch at the price. It has been so many years, and now you've learned to care about your money. Anyway, you deserve to be punished. So you select the very worst liquor you can find, the scuzziest off-brand whiskey. You buy the biggest bottle.

Hogan's is an accepting place. Welcoming, really. There are only alcoholics milling around when you carry your purchase to the register. How do you know they're alcoholics? It's your sixth sense. No one elbows anyone. No one smiles knowingly. They know you plan to go home and drink yourself into oblivion, and it's fine with them because that's what they're going to do, too. You can look the cashier in the eye and you can even pay with your bank card. You don't have to hand him two crumpled twenties and rush away, mumbling your thanks. You can smile and make small talk and sign your receipt with a flourish.

You get in your car and now you're excited. You hurry home, wash the dishes, walk the dog, complete all your daily chores. You decide not to eat dinner, because you will be more drunk on an empty stomach. You select a glass you almost never use, and decide that from now on, it will be your whiskey glass. You open the bottle, savor the smell. You pour two fingers, drink it. The whiskey is so cheap it burns, not in that good, clean, warm way, but with a painful scald.

You wait a minute. Five. There is nothing. Where is it?

You pour two more fingers. Then you add another two, for good measure. Choke it down. Ah. There it is. So good. That feeling! You wonder where it has been. I look and look for you, you think. Why is this the only place we meet?

You must have more. You do. More and more. Soon you are staggering through your apartment, cackling like a madman, because it's all so *funny*, then hushing when the ghost of your better self reminds you that you have neighbors, you should be quiet.

You drink and drink, forgetting altogether that you can't drink like you used to, that your body is wholly unaccustomed to alcohol. You drink like you used to drink, which is also the only way you know how to drink— fast and hard. *Power* drinking. You punish yourself.

Soon you are crying and maudlin. Who is this God, and what kind of God is he that he punishes you and abandons you? What have you done to deserve this? You are inconsolable. You sob and then you laugh. You try to get a box of tissues from the pantry, fall down, then get up and take them back to the bedroom, where you flop into the bed.

You pass out. You wake up six hours later and don't know what happened, although it's plain nothing did. Your dog looks at you, imploring you to walk him. He's waited so long. You have somehow become naked, so you put on green pants and a purple shirt and lurch outside with him. When you return, you realize you need to throw up. You turn off the bathroom light, kneel in front of the toilet, try to gag yourself. Nothing.

You go back to bed and fall into a dreamless half-sleep. You wake up every half hour or so, to look at the clock. You're too hot and you throw off your covers. There are books and papers strewn across your bed. How did they get there?

It's two o'clock. You begin to worry that you will still be drunk when you have to drive to work in a few hours. You walk to the kitchen, make a peanut butter sandwich in the dark, because the lights in the kitchen are too bright. You drink a liter of water—you are determined to push the fluids, flush out the alcohol.

Your body rebels. It doesn't want nourishment. You are back in front of the toilet, but now you are vomiting in earnest. You vomit so hard and for so long that it hurts, and you begin to worry you've wounded yourself, torn your guts into bloody ragged pieces.

Still, that felt better.

But now you're sick. Your stomach roils and burns.

The hours pass as painfully as kidney stones. You get out of bed at six. Shower. Make yourself eat. Drink some water. You convince yourself you are not still drunk.

You have to drive to work. What if you're wrong, if you're still drunk? You could kill someone. But you are pretty sure, mostly sure, fairly confident it's safe. You get in the car. There are cops everywhere, you think, and wouldn't they love to *get* you. You're paranoid, just like before, at the end.

You get to work and you're too sick to work. Too sick to stay, and too sick to go. You have to leave, drive home, all the way back again.

You're sick. So sick. You hate yourself for what you have become. For what you are. For being such a quitter. A failure. You think you will always remember how this feels. You'll never go back. This was the last time.

You take a nap. You wake up. You feel just a little bit better. You see the whiskey glass in the sink and you gag. You eat something.

And you start thinking of what's left in the bottle. This makes you nauseous, and it astounds you that you could want more.

But you do. You'd do it better this time. You wouldn't be such a pig about it. You'd drink less, and there wouldn't be such exquisite ecstasy, such fathomless despair. There would only be a steady buzz. Cool white pleasure, clean and constant.

Time is a construct, you say when you find yourself reaching for the bottle. What did all those days matter, if they already came and went and there is nothing more to do about them?

Ten years means nothing more than yesterday. There is only today. Today is worth more than all the rest of time put together, because it is here and it is real.

And then you pour another drink. It goes down easy.

The Bedroom Mirror

Anne Fox

In forty-five minutes, Emil, your new life. Check your tie, blue-on-blue silk, smooth under your finger. Secure the stickpin, the chip of diamond a point of morning light. Good, no tremble in the hand. Remember, it was not for Esther to ask, not for you to promise.

Trim the moustache. The feather-edge dust floats into your hand. Yes, you're a lucky man. It was a good life, you and Esther. But now, no more wondering. You can't know why she asked.

Put on your coat. A fine figure you cut—tall, thin, no stoop. No droopy eyelids. No floppy cheeks. No veins breaking under the skin. Still your own teeth. Yes, smile—you have the right. Tell yourself again.

Helen's watch on your wrist, platinum. Guaranteed for a lifetime. You laughed and asked, Whose lifetime? Helen didn't laugh. She put it in your hand, folded her fingers over yours. Esther's gold watch is already under the handkerchiefs in a drawer, the inscription—Esther to Emil—cut into the heart of the gold forever. Forever? It will stop ticking.

Whisk the shoulders. The pinstripe, a perfect fit. The handkerchief points exactly so in the breast pocket. Yes, check the fingernails.

Esther watches from her filigree-framed photograph on the dresser, her smile still mysterious. Don't forget the eyebrows. "John L. Lewis eyebrows," she called them.

Helen said, "Your eyebrows—striking with your white hair." She ran her finger over them.

Your promise to Esther broke at Helen's touch.

Take a good look. Admit it, you're a vain man. You learned long ago about silk ties and Paco Rabanne. They don't tailor-make sackcloth and ashes.

Smooth back your hair. The hat has to fit perfectly. Esther always liked you in a hat. She bought you every kind. She showed you off, all right. Remember the feel of her arm linked in yours, the lightness of her hand at your elbow?

Helen is a good-looking woman too. Your friends wink—lightning strikes twice.

Look at Esther's eyes in the photograph. You shake your head. Why that question, that whisper, her cold hand pressing yours? You still wonder about the wilderness of your promise. "No of course not, my darling, I never will."

And then Helen, illuminating a dark and lonely place.

The end of the world didn't come, did it?

Put on your hat, nudge the brim. Esther's eyes follow you around the room. She sees you feel in your pocket for the new wedding ring, your wallet, your keys. She sees your hand touch the frame. She doesn't know it's for the last time.

But you know it must be for the last time, don't you, Emil?

Take the photo, put it with the gold watch. Yes, put the past in the darkness of the drawer under the handkerchiefs along with the promise—an old, fragile promise.

Time to go. Tip your hat to the mirror, Emil, and walk out the door. Helen is waiting.

Are You Covered?
Carl Palmer

A day prior to your vacation, the letter arrives from the insurance company informing payment was not received.

Your online payment is confirmed by email receipt. All has occurred as always in the past several years.

The bank customer service representative says she will issue a new payment and void the original check.

Upon return you have an overpayment refund check in one envelope and a cancellation notice for nonpayment in the other.

The Fallen Leaves

Catherine Gracey

You push your chair away from your desk and stand up. The muscles in your back are stiff, and as you glance at the clock you realize you've worked through lunch without noticing. Again.

As you try to stretch out your aches you glance through the window. Outside the sky is clear and bright as the sun shines on the bronze and golden leaves that drift through your yard. It looks like a perfect day so close to winter, and you begin to wonder how you missed noticing the summer.

The computer chimes to announce another incoming email. You glance at it, suddenly resentful of all the hours you spend shut away in this room, the hours of overtime you have put in to impress a boss who doesn't care. Working from home was supposed to reduce the time you spent on this job, not increase it.

On impulse you grab your heavy coat and pull it on. You stuff your keys, phone and some money into a pocket. You take two steps towards the door before you take out your phone and toss it onto your desk. Let them call.

The breeze outside is cool but the sun is warm. You turn up your collar and consider going back for a scarf and gloves, but your feet keep walking away from the house.

You walk to a nearby park. There is a small café beside it, and you order a rich stew. Even this place has switched to their winter menu. The tables inside irritate you, so you take a vacant one outside. This spot is sheltered from the wind by the building, and as you wrap your cold hands around a steaming mug of caffeine you decide not to rush.

In the park someone has raked the fallen leaves into a large pile. Two small children play in them, tossing the leaves into the air and squealing with delight. You watch them as you eat, trying to recall the last time you felt so carefree and happy. How long has it been now?

The question plays in your mind as you trudge home. You continue to think about it as you unlock your door, as you see how many calls you missed, as you sit down and stare blankly at your computer. You're sure there must have been a time recently, but you can't remember.

You turn away from your desk and go back outside. You go to the shed and take out the rake. Carefully you collect every fallen leaf in the front yard. You carry them all into the back yard and continue cleaning there. The yard already looks better than it has for weeks.

When you are finished you realize you have worked out all the kinks in your back. You stretch, reveling in movement without stiff pain. It feels glorious.

Centered in the yard is a respectable pile of leaves. You set the rake aside. You take a deep breath and then jump on the pile. Leaves crackle under your shoes. You stomp your foot and the leaves scatter. It makes you grin.

You sit down in the pile and begin sweeping the leaves into the sky, the way the children were at the park. Leaves fall down around you, getting stuck in your hair and settling on your clothes. You brush some off and then stop yourself. Laughter escapes your lips and before long you are lying flat on your back, frantically moving your arms and legs as you try to make a leaf angel.

The back door opens and your partner walks outside to stare down at you. "What are you doing?"

A blush creeps across your cheeks, and you try to tell yourself it is just exertion and not embarrassment. "Um," you say as you sit up and survey the broken leaves around you. "I'm looking for something." It is the best you can come up with.

You expect a list of things you could be looking for: your mind, your sanity, your long lost youth. Instead of criticism your partner just nods and goes back inside. You stare at the closed door for several minutes until you start laughing.

Alone and happy again you finish your leaf angel. You brush as much mess from yourself as you can before going back inside. The air is getting cold with the setting sun, but knowing you relaxed enough to let go for a few hours is warming something you had not realized was so cold.

Shot of a Lifetime
Charlotte Jones

You saved for five years and traveled 10,000 miles for this moment. You came to Soliana Ranch, a private game preserve in Kenya, to photograph the largest of all land mammals. Here at Soliana you can walk, unlike in the National Parks that require you to ride in the safety of a vehicle. No aspects of civilization will spoil your pictures.

You trudge up the hill, the one overlooking the rocky outcrop that Disney recreated for The Lion King. While you catch your breath, you soak up the subtle pastels of the valley ahead, glowing in the African sunset. Disappointed that you've been out all day and have yet to see your elephant, you head back to camp.

Striding up the trail next to the cliff, along the forest edge, you suddenly hear a tremendous snap and then the slow crumbling crash of an acacia as it hits the ground. You cautiously venture around the next curve in the trail, expectations rising, and there he is. Thirteen feet tall at the shoulder, tusks close to eight feet long, the African bull elephant stands before you, 50 yards away, absorbed in making toothpicks of the once mighty tree.

You see him step on the fallen tree to hold it steady while he shreds off pieces of bark with his trunk. You hear his bone-breaking chewing, even from this distance. Holding your breath, so as not to be detected, you get your camera ready. This is the moment you have dreamed of, and you want everything to be perfect.

You crouch behind a tree and get your Nikon, setting the aperture on F8 and the shutter speed 1/60th of a second. You review all the other settings to ensure you are shooting Raw and the white balance is okay. You attach your flash, just in case, even though for now, the elephant is too far away. You hope to get close enough to use your flash to capture highlights in his eyes, to create that spark of life in your pictures.

You support your camera on the monopod you hauled in your pack. With your autofocus lens, you compose the picture you've dreamed of. The camera frames the elephant's head and torso, the horizontal light of the late afternoon sun accentuates every wrinkle, every feature of this magnificent beast.

Click Perfect, you think as you quietly move a little closer. Click. The light makes the elephant's skin look like burnished copper. Click. You're close enough now for fill flash to ensure that no detail is lost in the shadows cast by the golden orange-red of the sky. Click.

The elephant stops chewing and turns his head slowly in your direction.

Click. The light is so perfect, so beautiful, even his eyelashes stand out. Click. Good, you think. Come on, baby, and look straight into the camera. Pose for me. Click.

The elephant raises his trunk, testing the night air.

Perfect. Click. God, you think, what great pictures these will be. Click. You adjust the shutter speed. Slower will add a sense of action to your pictures by slightly blurring the elephant's movement. Click.

Enraptured in the moment of making perhaps your best pictures ever, you fail to notice that the elephant has now noticed you. Click. His six-foot-long ears stand out, a clear warning sign to those more skilled in animal behavior. Click. The elephant shakes his head and stamps his feet. Click. Small clouds of dust rise from the ground and from the shuddering skin on his back. Click. Click.

At the first rumble of the elephant's threatening trumpet, his final warning before flattening his ears against his lowered head and charging, you finally notice.

Click.

The severity of your situation dawns on you. Elephant ahead. Forested hill to the right. Cliff to the left. No place to go. No gun. Oh. God. You feel the ground shake as the elephant charges. You throw your camera, monopod and pack in the direction of the elephant, as if that can stop him, and run like hell down the hill. You smell the hot breath of the animal briefly before the 150,000 muscles in his trunk coordinate to crush your ribs. You feel the searing pain while his tusk punctures your left kidney. You scream as your feet leave the ground, your last conscious expression.

Full flashes in the control panel of your camera, as it lies hidden in the brush with your best pictures, the pictures that will never be seen be seen by anyone, including your spouse back at camp who begged you to please, please take a guide and a gun.

Canyons
C.S. Cole

The sky is supposed to be full of birds you would
expect in a gray Pacific Northwest winter with flutters of
drab olive and flashes of ivory. You would nod and jot
notes in your birding journal like a general critiquing
strafing runs. And you would smile when a new variety
visits the myriad of feeders hanging from your neighbor's
balcony just across the concrete canyon; the balcony
almost close enough to reach if not for the twenty-floor
drop, and the restraining order not to do so.

The feeders sway empty. You haven't seen a new
bird in weeks, the few there returning out of habit in hopes
of finding a sliver of seed, a smudge of suet, an unwary
bug.

Maybe your neighbor is off on holiday, somewhere
back east visiting family, bundled up together in a drafty
farmhouse sipping coffee and eggnog in front of a
crackling fire in a worn brick fireplace built before the
revolution. Conversation would hem and haw over the trip
and the weather, and then rush headlong onto legal
battles and other ugly things, and the aforementioned
beverages would be exchanged for something much
stronger.

You could have gone with her had you not professed your fear of flying, and of snow. You could have taken something for your nerves, made a joke of it, and not been such a jerk with your concerns. At least you wouldn't be spending the winter alone with your obsession on counting dull Pine Siskin and chatty Chickadee while she makes a go of it alone.

Movement catches your attention and you raise your binoculars in time to catch a sight that almost brings a gasp to your lips.

You gasp anyway.

She is so thin, as thin as a bird, you think.

Your neighbor is there behind the thick glass of her balcony door, naked except for your lawyer's blue-tinged stationary pressed to her eyes. She's crying, sobbing, her shoulders heave up and down and her chest caves inward. If you could, you would look away to allow her privacy but you can't.

You never played a caring role before. Why start now?

So you step back and hide behind the long strands of a dead houseplant abandoned when she moved out and away, yet not far away and in fact, to the only apartment available in the entire city, which just happened to be located in the high-rise building straight across from the life she left.

You were indifferent about it. Go, you said, do what you will. And you fluttered your hand, your fingers as if wings in flight.

A flurry advances and you see the birds have been replaced by snow; huge, sloppy flakes swirling between the buildings, squeezing the air from your lungs, blurring the view of your once-beloved.

Lord no, not snow, you whisper.

The world turns white, white like the light at birth, the light at death, the white of her skin, the whites of her eyes.

She is outside now and you stare at the flakes melting on her pale shoulders. She is crying and maybe she needs fresh air. Unconsciously, you inhale deeply and wait for her to do the same. Bloodless knuckles clutch the metal railing instead, your letter whipped by the wind becomes a plane, a parachute, a precursor.

She looks across the chasm and smiles. Her lips move and it hits you she's smiling because she doesn't see you and you clasp a hand over your mouth to keep from giggling. You hold your side as the laughter gives way to teary-eyed hysterics.

Where else would you be?

"Don't want to miss anything," you said, binoculars and journal in hand, day in and day out. "Things happen."

Here's the proof. It's obvious.

She must be thinking of you, unless she's thinking of visiting her family. She was happiest then and mused why you weren't the same.

"Snow," you said, justifying everything, explaining nothing. "And flight," you said, shutting off the matter.

What is she trying to tell you now, smiling, crying, standing naked twenty floors above the city? You look for a glimmer of recognition and see, perhaps, a nod. You know then, she sees you but what is she repeating over and again?

And why would you care?

Snow and flight.

Suicide.

From the distance, the words upon the lips both look the same. She always knew what got to you.

The birds launch into a prelude.

You dare to raise the binoculars to your eyes and find the lenses have fogged. By the time you dab them with a corner of your robe, a corner of your eye catches a wave. She must be telling you she's going.

Go, you shout.

No, you scream.

From a distance, a scream and a shout both sound the same.

The snow parts for a moment and the sky is filled with bird.

And you realize for the last time, flight is beautiful.

Push
David Ballard

In dreams, your father does not have cancer.

The two of you are flying kites in this dream, and you are five again. You clap your hands and giggle as the shimmering gold kites leap from the ground, their endless knotted tails whispering complex patterns in the sky. Your father runs across the field with his line and you try to keep up with him, to be like him, to chase the wind and fly with him. As is weird in dream logic, the kites lift you both up into the sky, carrying you higher and higher into the clouds as the buildings below shrink away.

Then the telephone rings. As you answer it, the wind from your dream disappears into the receiver.

It's your father.

"I'm ... sorry I woke you up. This is important."

"Dad...?"

And then you realize the wind really is in the telephone, that it's blowing wherever your father's calling from. He's probably on his cell phone.

"Please. I need you to come down to the new Provident Building right now. Corner of High and Sixth. I'll be on the top floor. There's a key in the hoist for you."

You look at the alarm clock next to your small bed. The kites have now disappeared, the sparkling tips of their tails winking out of the corner of your eye. It's 3:16 a.m.

"Corner of ... you mean downtown? Now?"

"Please. It's very important."

"Dad? Are you sick? Do you need a ride –?"

"No, no. Nothing like that. I just need your help with something. Please come now."

And he hangs up.

What is there to do? So you dress quickly, drive about eighty through the deserted streets leading downtown, and replay the telephone call in your mind.

I need your help with something.

Your father rarely needs help with anything. He never even told anybody about the lump in his groin until his second week of chemotherapy, and then only after he had quit that and refused any further treatment because it turned him "into a goddamn walking zombie."

He didn't sound upset or afraid over the phone, or even mad for that matter. What could be so important?

You park next to your dad's Jeep in front of his construction trailer. There are no other vehicles around. It's warm for the middle of September, but you grab your windbreaker from the back of your Honda and slip it on. The gate in the perimeter fence is open. Next to what will be the foyer of this half-finished skyscraper there is a note taped to the panel in the service elevator. Please come to the top floor.

As the hoist grinds its way up and carries you higher, the steepled tops of the older buildings around you shrink away. This new giant, nearly forty stories so far, has a feeling of power to it even though it is less than half finished. The wind is colder now as it whistles through the open sides, so you zip up your jacket.

You have been coming to the buildings your father designed since you were a toddler. He used to dangle you upside-down over the edges of the city, his strong arms like cables you knew would never let you go, and you would squeal out Do it again, Daddy! Do it again! as he swung you out and over the city, upside-down. You could never get enough of that.

When you slide both lift gates open at the top, there sits your dad, leaning against a beam, drinking a Diet Pepsi. Even though he's lost more weight and the veins in his hands and neck seem bigger, he still looks vital in his denim shirt, jeans and boots, and then it hits you what really looks different about the scene, other than the fact that it's night.

He's not wearing his construction helmet.

"Thanks," he says. "I wasn't sure you'd come."

"Sure, Dad. What's going on? What are you doing up here now?"

"I'm going to jump off this building tonight."

This time the wind roars from within you, and you cannot breathe. All you can think to say is no! but the breath won't come. Is he serious? Is he crazy? My God, this is all rushing in way too fast. Seeing this, he answers the questions you cannot ask.

"It's spread from my colon into my liver, and it's too late to stop it from getting worse. It's just now started to hurt like hell. I've got two months, six at the outside. I've seen what it does and I don't want to die like that."

This is still coming way too fast.

"This is Bob Hartzell. I met him at the hospice, and he's got it worse than me. Over there's his son, Amos."

You had not even noticed anyone else up here, and now you see them, near the edge of the east platform just outside the glow of one of the overhead bulbs. The older one is stooped with his hands in his coat pockets, his eyes sunken and bruised. His skin has a yellowish cast under the light. His clothes look tired and gray.

Amos is much bigger, fat even, leaning against a wall and devouring a Baby Ruth candy bar. He does not look at his father. Instead he wipes his greasy hands on his sweatshirt and smiles, looking you in the eyes briefly, then dropping his gaze to look you up and down. He's creepy, this fat guy, with small pig eyes and a wet mouth.

"Dad, I—"

"Bob is jumping, too. We both left notes in our cars explaining everything, so nobody has to worry about ... consequences."

Each word punches, magnifying the chill that begins at the back of your head and now creeps into your face. Before you can take another breath, he hits you with the zinger.

"I want you to push me."

*

Now I lay me down to sleep
I say a prayer before I leap
And if I die before I wake...
No wait a minute, dammit, that's not right...
And lead us not to temptation
But deliver us from evil
Our Father ... Our Father ...
Our Father who art in Heaven...
Oh, Christ
Oh, sweet Jesus Christ, did he say..
Breathe.
Breathe.
Breathe.
Did he really say he wanted me to—
?

*

"You want me to do what?"

Your dad exhales and turns to the two Hartzell men, as if all of them had expected this response. Bob and Amos turn away, like there could really be any privacy on this open, windy platform of an unfinished floor. Your dad stands and walks toward the edge to face the quiet city below.

"I've been up here every night for the past week," he says, "but I couldn't do it myself. Bob came up the past two nights. We stood here on this platform, wanting to take that step, and neither of us could let go."

"That's not what I'm talking about," you say. "Why? Why are you up here?"

Your father grips the flange of an upright steel beam next to him with his right hand and slowly swings out over the edge. God, he's going to do it right now. You've seen him do this a thousand times, just swing out over the drop like that, but this time he might just let go and do it right now in front of you. But he doesn't. He sways there, moored to the beam, his elbow creaking, and then swings back around the other side to face you.

"I've been beaten by this," he finally says. "I've seen how they die in the hospitals, and it smells like decay in there. It's so vile and stifling you have to breathe through your mouth. Except by the time I get there, my mouth will be taped around a tube, and everything hooked up to a screen or a bottle. I need you to help me."

"No!"

"I believe you can."

"Dad – it's murder."

"Yes," he says, and for the first time he scratches his chin, considering this. "I suppose it is."

You both talk.

A crescent moon emerges in the west, and while you talk, it rises up into the clouds, where it peeks out now and then, checking in to see if the city below is still asleep. There is no ceiling here – you are on the top of the world.

You talk about dreams, and going after them. You talk about pain, and helplessness. About Easter Egg hunts and Christmas wishes granted or long forgotten. You talk about destiny, about promises, about unfulfilled potential, about eternity. You talk about dying, and what comes next. It is your talk, between you and your Dad, and you talk about everything for what seems like forever, everything except what has brought you here.

"Please," he says. "You know I can't ask your brother to do this. You know how upset he gets."

"I'm not going to push you off this building."

"And your mother's out, since she's afraid of heights."

"Dad!"

"You're the only one who can help me," he says, looking into your eyes. "I know you can do this. Just to get me started. Just to help me let go. Just to keep me from standing there, one more time, praying I had the nerve just to take that one tiny step!"

All three of them are watching you, waiting for you to decide, each probably thinking that if you leave, they will never get another chance. The whole thing will be over. Even the wind whispering through the beams seems to plead come on, it's getting late, do this for your old man, just one push, a small one, for your dad.

You look over at Bob Hartzell, and he rises and shuffles to the edge of the platform. As if on cue, Amos snorts and dutifully marches directly behind his father.

If your dad stands now, you're leaving, that's it.

But he waits. He drinks from a Diet Pepsi and your stomach burns as he winces.

Oh, God.

You close your eyes and stand, breathing calmly but shaking inside all the same. The wind is stronger now. You open your eyes and blow out a long breath, and walk to the edge of the platform. Do it now, quick, before you have a chance to change your mind.

Amos practically ogles you as you walk over – God, what could possibly be on his mind? He thrusts out his hand and says, "Nice to meet you."

"Fuck off, Amos."

Embarrassed, as if he had just greeted a one-armed guest, Amos wipes his grubby hand on his stained sweatshirt and steps back away from you.

You can hear your father rising to his feet, and you clamp your eyes shut again and grab onto the beam for balance. From behind he hugs you hard, as he always did when you ran from monsters who lunged from the dark closets or under the basements stairs. You turn around and hug him back. He squeezes you so hard you can hardly breathe. So you don't. If you don't breathe and he keeps squeezing, the moment will last, forever, don't let it stop.

Off to the side, Bob and Amos just look at the floor, as if one is afraid to touch the other. Your father releases you then, and without looking back, he walks over to stand next to Bob near the edge. Amos steps behind his father and flexes his fingers – pushing position, no doubt. If someone could see the four of you now from a distance, it might look like the beginning of a midnight sled race at the top of a snowy hill, lit only by the moon and warmed by childhood anticipation.

It is agreed, muttered actually, that after the count of three you will both push. Not one-two-push, but one-two-three-then-push. Right. Got it.

I say a prayer before I leap.

You look at your dad's broad back, outlined only by the stars.

"One."

You breathe in, deeply, and smell the eternal Dad-smell of aftershave and sweat, the way he always smelled when he came home for dinner.

"Two."

When you put your hands on his trembling back, they are the small hands of a five-year-old pressing into Daddy's middle, trying to get him to budge on the playground swing and only sinking into the warm, foam rubber padding that is Daddy.

"Three."

You gently push those child's hands with the muscles of an adult, and you feel this giant redwood toppling away from your fingertips. When his weight gets away, the fingers in your mind clench tight and hold, but the fingers of your hands in front of you are outstretched and rigid. Through them you see only a fluttering shirttail flapping furiously in the wind as it disappears down into the darkness.

You hear Amos before you notice them both still standing there.

"I'm sorry, Daddy! I just couldn't do it! Please don't make me do it, Daddy! I can't! I just can't!"

What the –?

You reel and glare at them both, you can't believe this! You swallow it down, but it burns, it burns, and finally you get the breath to scream, "I WAS AGAINST THIS ALL ALONG!"

You can still hear the fluttering of your father's shirttail, like kite tails whipping in the wind, as you push them both over the edge.

George II
David Malone

Arrive early on a grey-stained morning at the café she has chosen. Press your face against the locked glass door. Inside, faux-Italian baristas are circling, fanning out napkins on freshly- laid tablecloths. Rap at the glass until one heads your way. Smile as the door opens. Say: "I guess I'm the early bird," and step inside, scouring the room for a suitable spot. Opt for a corner- table with a view of the entrance. Ignore the menu and prepare for scenarios: imagine her fainting; do not rule out vomiting. She is your wife. It has been more than six months.

She appears from nowhere, like Joan Bennett in film noir. Watch as she surrenders her coat, revealing a gold-leafed dress that shimmers as she walks. Her hair is up. She's lost some weight. Search the tablecloth for the right sentence. Strike a chord between familiarity and reverence: the lovechild of 'Hey Baby!' and 'Dearest One." Glance up as she sits. Break the ice and say:

"Your mother's going to love hell."

A muscle twitches in her left cheek. The lines in her neck could be the root of a smile. Follow it down to her chest instead; a delta of cracking skin where Christ on a cross hangs, lopsided, nestled in cleavage.

"George," She purrs, leaning forward to pet your hand; your silly, insignificant little hand, "You are her hell."

*

"The university named a scholarship after you," She tells you, as coffee is served from a carafe. "It went to a Chinese PhD student: 'Jonathan Hou from Guangzhou.' That's how he introduced himself to the board of governors: like a rhyming couplet for them all to remember."

Wonder why this is important. Reach for her hand and miss.

"They sent him home after your 'resurrection.' Budgets, they said."

And note the bareness of her fingers as she draws them back: long and slender; a librarian's fingers.

"Can't hand out a live man's dead scholarship!" She half-laughs, filling up the space between your faces.

Stare at her face as she looks out the window.

"Nobody knows how to handle the fact that you're back. They sent that boy home with a suitcase full of broken dreams. I said it wasn't fair, but Alan wouldn't have it. He said you were back and it changed the university's charter, changed the rules, changed everything really."

A chirping sound, like a chorus of trapped crickets, halts her stream of thought. Watch as she lifts and unfastens her handbag; presses a couple of buttons on her new phone; takes a moment to read the message; smiles, then un-smiles.

"My friend." she says, without having to add any more.

"How is he?" you ask, right letters, wrong order. Clever you.

"He's good; happier now he's past the bar." She assures you, as she tucks her phone under a napkin.

Take the biscotti from her saucer, snap it in half, dunk it. Say: "So he's a child then?"

"He's a Professor!" she corrects you, smacking the table with her ring-less hands. "He sails!"

Do not be surprised by this. Some women lust for firemen; most lust for abusive firemen. She drips for academics.

"You said he'd passed the bar?"

"The bar; yes, the bar! The bar at the mouth of the river! He's racing to Douglas, to the Isle of Man."

Isle of Man, Isle of Men, I love Men. Let it warp in your ears. Say: "You didn't wait long, Anita"

Her face turns as long and as blank as the future. It reminds you of a child resigned.

"Long?" She asks.

Nod. Roll the question around in your mouth like a bitter pill. Spit it back out: "You left me behind."

"You were dead, George. You died." She states plainly.

Bat her assertions away until she wrestles your hand down. "There was a funeral; there was cake for Christ's sake!"

Know that life is a line that can be smudged, that you love her, that it was ever so. Slip your fingers between hers and ask:

"Would you rather I was still in the ground, dear?"

The look she gives you is barbarous: a cold reminder of the girl you un-caged all those years ago.

"I think it's good that you're back," She says, using the word good in a severely technical manner. "I don't understand this—I can't—but I know it's important."

Tell her you can take her some place new, like she always wanted. Somewhere far away from this maritime backwater; a place where the salt isn't everywhere, creeping up the walls.

She throws her napkin over your half-full cup, and then motions for the bill. "Peter warned me this might be too soon," She murmurs.

Feel the adrenaline fizzing up behind your eyes. That name.

"Peter the rock, your other professor."

The ten pound note she presses to the table pitches up, and collapses again, as she scrambles for her bag.

Despite yourself, ask for his specialty.

"Not that it matters —" She sighs, zipping it up, "— but he's a social anthropologist." Laugh so loud that a waitress across the room breaks step, and pivots with her tray. "You find this funny?" she asks.

"He's good, George. He's helped me see—"

Give her some perspective. Blast the windows open: "Does he fuck my wife like a native, or a settler!?" "He loves me."

"I love you more."

Her fingers flick the words away before they can take root.

Pull yourself back from the edge. Scratch an ear with your teaspoon and wait.

"I keep asking myself if I'm dreaming awake, how you can possibly be here. Every day the same damn merry-go-round! Do you know what they're calling you in the newspapers? Have you even looked at one? You won't speak to anyone, so they're filling in the blanks for you.

They're calling you 'George, the Second.'

"You've given people a false hope. They started leaving their jobs in the middle of the day. They started digging up their loved ones. The army had to step in while you just sat there in your hospital bed, refusing to talk, devouring pot after pot of pudding like a starved mute!"

Tell her you like pudding; it is not a crime to like pudding.

"Joan dug her cats up in her garden—I caught her in the act—and do you know what she said to me? She told me to fuck off, that it was just in case."

Change the subject. Ask of her mother.

"My mother doesn't believe any of this!" She barks. "It's not possible to her; you're just a blip – that's how she sees it. She calls you The Burp of God."

Grin at the image. Lean in and say: "He hears everything, you know."

Watch as her personal saviour rises up from the mounds of her chest. Anticipate the question as she rubs his feet with her thumb. Stand. Tap your wedding ring against the glass of the carafe. Announce:

"Death is like being alone in a room with a coke machine!"

It echoes off the walls as she slumps, like an abandoned concertina, further down into her seat.

"I know it doesn't sound like much, but that's what it's like. It isn't grand; there are no trumpet-calls, no angels. Just a humming and humming and humming through everything; stretching you out in all directions forever and ever, Amen."

The room is silent now, save for the fast clicking of a waitresses heels rushing toward you: her face a squinted tangle of embarrassment and duty.

"Sir," She insists. "Sir, this is yours."

Take the slip of carbon paper from between her fingers and sit. Lean back, casual-like, hooking your arm around the back of the seat. Breathe in the sweet-smelling air and say:

"My wife, isn't she something? I've known her for thirty years. I know that probably sounds like a lot to you, but let me assure you it isn't. The truth is we hardly had time to feel happy, then sad together."

She is patting her lips with a napkin as you talk, looking off at the wallpaper.

"She's the only woman I've ever slept with, apart from a hooker in Crete. I know that sounds bad, but the truth often is. It pushed us together in the long-run: set a little fire under us that never went away. Every year she'd fight her way back to it, like a salmon, ready for the struggle and the sex of it. It exhausted and renewed us. It became an anniversary of sorts. You won't know this, young lady, but old bodies slip when they make love."

"You're embarrassing the girl," she tells you as she signals another waiter for her coat. Shrug at her momentary discomfort. Say:

"I love the body you live in."

She is nodding now, lifting a thumb energetically as the right coat is selected and unhooked. The vinyl floor groans beneath her as she steps past you, and into it.

"There's an order to things, George" she says, buttoning herself up to the tip of her chin. "It may not matter to you, but it matters to me. Take that away from people and you leave them with nothing."

Catch her cuff as she makes for the door. She lurches forward and gasps at the tug; the involuntary twirl spins her back to you like the beginning of a dance. Drop to your knees and squeeze her waist. Push your face into her stomach and tell her something true. Say:

"There is more than one kind of emptiness, Anita."

She glances down at you, rubs her fingers through your brittle hair. Quietly responds: "You can come by the house for what's left; there isn't much."

Feel her slipping away from you, smooth as a ship launching, as she heads for the door, then out into the street, tightening her coat against the knifing wind. The skirt of it swings as she walks away, rocking behind her like a Sunday bell.

For the longest of moments it is all you can see.

Animal Songs

Gale Martin

When you grow up on a farm with a big pond on the property and the windows hang open six months out of the year—no air conditioning—you are serenaded by animals. You come to expect peeping and croaking and cooing to lull you to sleep, to remind you warm weather's arrived, even before you are old enough know which animals sing which songs.

Each spring after the sun goes to bed, the music begins with an invisible chorus of creatures chirping. You think it's a million crickets scratching their hairy legs together.

"Those are spring peepers," your dad says the next day when your head is drooping into your cereal bowl and you have to explain why you couldn't fall asleep.

And you'll never forget that sound, no matter where you live for the rest of your life, a musical kind of crackling—like sandpaper if sandpaper could sing. Then one day you are eight, trying to catch tadpoles in a Mason jar, and you see a frog no longer than an inch worm, and you tell your dad about the little fellow you found today.

He says, "That's a spring peeper."

And you think how funny it is that a miniature frog has musical sandpaper in his throat, so much that he can keep you awake for hours each night unless your body's plum worn out from riding your bike to the orchard and back. Once in a while, you hear the bellows of bullfrogs, sounding like frogs are supposed to, like hearing the kettle drums in an orchestra. Bullfrogs have hiding places all around the pond, so you never see them croaking from that big bulge in their gaping mouths. But who doesn't know the song of bullfrogs, right?

Same thing for the mourning doves, who toddle all over your lawn and your flowerbeds, hunting seeds. You think maybe it's all the thistle seeds giving them their lonesome song, like chickens who eat marigold seeds and their meat turns yellow. You think surely mourning doves have the most beautiful song of any bird. Well, what about the mockingbird, you ask? Just a noisy overachiever, the mockingbird is, plain and simple.

If not the prettiest bird, then mourning doves have the most plaintive song. Your heart hurts a little, each time you hear their lonesome cooing, especially when you're thirteen and rocking in the front porch glider by yourself.

Then you are fifteen, almost sixteen. Your heart is swollen, ready to explode, because a really smart, popular boy in the twelfth grade drives you home after school. You sit outside your house in the early evening in his blue Maverick, killing time, until he works up the nerve to kiss you. All of sudden the mourning dove sings its sorrowful song. He hears that sad "cooOOO, coo, coo, coo" and asks whether that was a groundhog singing.

"No, silly," you say because he's a city kid, even though he's like a genius. Or at least that's what your friends have said. "Groundhogs don't sing. It's a little brown dove. Haven't you ever seen a mourning dove?"

But you let him kiss you anyway because you've loved him almost since the school year started, but he only noticed you last week. And you feel good that you can teach him about animal songs. But not as good as when he finally kisses you.

Mirror Gate

Herika R. Raymer

You step down from the bus and are immediately assailed by the stale popcorn, warm cotton candy, and rotten food smell of the fair. Only instead of it repulsing you, there is a flair of excitement that takes you. After all, it is only once a year that your school lets out to allow its students to attend the fair during its brief stop to your town.

It was always the same. The fair came to town, and every school allowed only one day for the students to attend. It was a given that weekends would be over-crowded, and parents usually worked during the week, so as a show of good faith the districts would allow the teachers to escort their classes there during one day of the week. You always thought it was a waste. Not of money or time, since your parents did become somewhat generous on Fair Day and it was always nice to have a break from the endless droning of facts, tests, and reviews.

It was more a waste of a good vacation day in your opinion. Normally Fair Day was either incredibly hot and muggy or overcast with either drizzling rain or a straight downpour. Today, however, the sky was clear and the weather was unusually mild. You had come prepared for foul weather dressed in comfortable jeans, old but reliable running shoes, a thin long sleeved shirt with a short sleeve cotton shirt underneath in case you needed to lose the outer shirt, and a light denim jacket with the arms tied around your waist. Heck, the back pack you always carried had a towel and a change of clothes among your usual stash of a minor first aid kit, some pouches of dried edibles, and a few bottles of water.

As you gather with the others to pass through the Fair Entrance, you feel a giddy excitement that demands you explore. Other outings had been to museums, galleries, and the usual educational outposts. Yet this, this was something that appeals to the inner child, awakening it, and enticing it to run free. The sounds of the games are calling to you, the rickety sounds of the ride machinery makes your heart beat faster in excitement, the bright colors of the flyers and the prizes is almost overpowering, and now the aroma of food is more appetizing rather than revolting. You begin to dance on the balls of your feet, eager to get started.

Your backpack digs into your flesh, so you shrug the straps to readjust the weight. The answering giggles from some of your classmates did not bother you. The daily teasing for your peculiar practice had long since faded to a insect-like drone in your ears. It was interesting that, on days like this when your classmates got hungry before mealtime and had run out of money no one laughed at you but instead were your best friend. You shudder as you recall that one miserably hot day when several students had come to you, piteously asking for food. Not hungry yourself, and thinking it could do no harm, you decided to share what little provisions you carried. Initially it had been ok, but then word spread you had food and was passing it out. Before long, your rations were depleted and there were still hungry mouths begging for food. When they found out there was nothing more to give, the attitude towards you had become ugly. The name calling was terrible, but it was the least of it. You had been pushed and pulled as the students pulled the backpack from you and ravaged the innards, while trying to see if you had stashed anything in your own pockets. Thankfully the adults had been paying attention and managed to rescue you and your belongings before too much damage was done. You were bruised and frightened, but not too terribly hurt. Still, the experience had been enough to ensure you always carried double portions on outing days such as this, not to mention you kept close to your real friends or to an adult.

Here though, you feel energized, invincible. You can almost hear the voices telling you to explore outside your usual safety zones. Perhaps this wasn't such a waste after all.

The first games are a flurry of movement and laughter. You Pan For Gold and then go to the Shooting Gallery, then top it off at the Basketball Toss. It is so much fun just to be able to cut loose. Naturally, you do not win anything, but you are having too much fun to care.

The time comes to begin the rides. As always, you avoid the roller coasters as the immediate draw. Instead you ride the Helicopter first, followed by the Spider, and the Sky Rocket. The adrenaline has energized you enough to help you brave the roller coasters, and you and your friends delight in screaming as the cars sped along their aerial tracks. Afterward, the lull of the energy spent has you making your way to the Hall of Mirrors.

Giggling as you make odd faces in the warped reflective surfaces, you and your friends idly play. It takes a few moments before you realize that there is prickling at the base of your neck. The silent signal of unease had begun as a slight discomfort, but was building to an unreachable itch. Even as you massage the area, the sensation will not quit.

You and your friends are near the center of the display, jostling and taunting one another. You are distracted for only a moment, trying to figure out why you are so uncomfortable. The pushing of your neighbors tips you off balance and you teeter, falling backwards, and bracing yourself to hit the hard surface of the tall mirror.

Only the impact never happens.

You continue to fall, well past where the mirror should have stopped you. Before you know it, you are on the ground. For a moment you are confused, looking up at the ceiling. Then you look around, trying to find out why you did not land against the mirror.

The shocking sight of multiple columns of broken mirrors snaps you to attention.

Rolling onto your hands and knees, you hear the crunch of glass beneath your weight. It is enough to cause you tread with more caution, since you do not want to cut yourself. Easing onto your feet, you look around and see nothing but shattered reflections. The tinge at your neck falls to your stomach, souring it.

"Hello?" you cringe as your voice echoes through the empty corridors.

Empty.

Realization hits you then that you do not hear anything. No traffic. No voices. No machinery. Nothing. You are alone.

Panicked, you manage to make your way out of the ruined Hall of Mirrors and find yourself witness to an even more terrifying sight. The abandoned expanse of the Fair stretches before you. The rides look even more neglected than usual. There is trash everywhere, but there is no accompanying stench. You sniff the air, but there is no scent. Reaching over to the nearest stall you pick up something, anything, and sniff it. Nothing. Again you pick an item up off the ground. Nothing. No scent. It bothers you that there is not even a scent of decay. What is worse, as you handle some wrapping paper you do not hear the usual crinkle of the material. No sound. That is when you look around and see the idle swinging of some of the dangling swings and realize that you do not hear the mechanical squeaks either. The Fair here may look the same, the same colors and layout, but there is no smell or sound to this place and it looks as though it is ready to fall apart.

"Hello!" you call out, shuddering as your voice echoes again. "Is there anyone here?"

Running from booth to booth, you look for any sign of life. Unfortunately there is nothing. Not even the skittering of vermin. It is an indication of your rising alarm that even that would be welcome right now. Only there is no evidence of cockroaches, rats, or other scavengers that usually accompany Fairs, feasting on the leftover food thrown aside by the patrons. Except that she could see the spoiling food, just not the creatures that feasted on them. You are truly alone.

There is no one here that you remember. No friends, no teachers, no family. There are not even any of the animals you would welcome. No birds, no stray dogs, no parasites. It is even odd that you miss the mechanical sounds of the Fair, the motorized roar of the traffic, and the annoying ringing of cell phones.

You cannot help it as you begin to cry. A sorrow fills you as you realize you are in a strange place, with no one to guide you, and no certain way to get back. Hell, you are not even certain how you got here to start with!

Your cries reverberate off of the surfaces around you, magnifying the sound and making it worse. You want to stop the terrible sound, but even hearing the misery you are in troubles you further. To sound so hopelessly lost, so terribly alone, you never knew you could make such a heartbreaking sound.

It must have been that which called the Thing to you.

Luckily, you heard it well before it found you.

It was the sound that pulled you out of your misery. The distant thumping interrupted your wails. The rhythmic cadence approached where you sat, the sound resembling the eerie pounding from a haunted house film. Through tear-blinded eyes, you looked around. Unfortunately, you could not see anything. Even when you wiped your eyes, there was nothing to see on the clear day. And still the sound got closer, and you could begin to feel the ground vibrate with each thump.

Whatever it was, it was huge. A primal fear takes hold of you, prompting you to stumble towards a nearby booth to hide. As you cower there, you become aware of an aroma. A terrible one approaches, heavy and sterile and not unlike the acrid smell of a hospital. Not the sweet cloying reassuring scent either, but the intense and burning scent that calls to mind sickness and death. It is so fierce you have to cover your nose and mouth with your hands. It makes your eyes water, it is so strong, and you are grateful that you had not eaten before going on the rides as bile creeps up your throat. A morbid curiosity takes you, causing you to wonder what could possibly be so big and smell so bad. As you squeeze the tears from your eyes, you realize that the air is becoming misty. The ground beneath you shakes as the Thing arrives, the stench overpowering, and the mist thickening into a fog. You realize that even if you wanted to, you would not be able to see it. The realization brings with it a bit of sense, even if you were able to see it what would you do? You do not know what it is, if it is friendly, or if it would help you.

Backing further into the shadows of the booth, you watch as the fog literally cascades down the table above you. You are grateful for the box hiding you but allowing for a bit of sight. Not that you could see anything, since you could feel the thing moving behind you. The sound of something impossibly large, moving around, searching the booths, causes you to try and make yourself even smaller. Facing the back of the booth, you see the shadow creep over the boards as it gets closer, and accompanying the sight is a chill. Not just because you are afraid, but because it has gotten colder. The frost following the shadows as they cover things does not help your terror either. Though the cold bites at you, you dare not move to put your jacket on properly.

The sound has gotten even closer, if that is possible. It is like hearing yourself moving around in a box, every twist and turn made magnified and incredible. As if the sound, smell, darkness, and cold were not enough, now there is something else - something almost tangible. A maliciousness that you can feel radiating from the thing as it searches the Fairgrounds. That malice keeps you hidden until, after an agonizing long time, it moves on. You do not know why it cannot find you, as you are sure you are as different to this place as it is, but you are grateful.

The haze remains, indicating to you that it has not gone far, but the vibrations of its movements is a thrum now. Cautiously, you peer out. It does not surprise you that the Fairgrounds are now covered in a layer of ice. Pulling your jacket from your waist, you put it on and look around. The fright from the hatred you sensed has not left you, it has only told you that you have to get out of here. Except the question is how.

Settling back down in your hiding spot, you look in your backpack. There is nothing there that looks like it can help. Searching the side pockets, you desperately pull out your identification, a brush, a mirror, and a lighter. You clench your teeth as you feel your throat tighten, threatening to voice another sob. Looking at your reflection in the small mirror, it never occurred to you that terror could be so visceral as to change your entire appearance. You look nothing like yourself with wild eyes set in a pale and drawn face. You reach out to touch the mirror...

... and are startled when your fingers go through! You look at it for a moment, and then pull your fingers back. Incredulous, you look at your fingers and try again. Once more they pass through the glass surface. Hope surges through you as you realize you just might have found a way out.

Of course! If you got here through a mirror, then a mirror had to be your way out. Just as quickly, the hope dampens. All you recall of the ones in the Hall of Mirrors is that they were shattered. There had to be a way to find a mirror that was big enough to get you out. Should you search the other booths? No, no. That would leave you vulnerable to whatever was out there.

Wait! Pictures on your cell phone taken during the first part of the day, you and your friends had posed in many of the thoroughfares. Perhaps that could help you find a mirror without leaving the safety of your refuge. Yet as you dig the technology out of your jacket pocket and scan through the images, you hope is dwindling fast. There was nothing in the pictures to indicate that there was another large mirror anywhere. Only in the Hall of Mirrors.

You lean back against the booth wall with your knees up and your head on your knees. There had to be a way out, and you were relatively certain it was there. If only you could puzzle out how to make it back to your own world.

Wait. Puzzle.

Your head comes up abruptly as you realize that broken mirrors usually could be pieced back together. There were cracks, yes, but a full mirror could be remade. If you could remake one of the mirrors, even if just by half, it might be enough to get you out.

The acrid antiseptic smell returned, prompting you to hide again. The Thing was making rounds on the Fairgrounds, looking for you. It had heard you, and knew you were there. Running your fingers through your loose hair, you try to think of what to do. After all, getting glass pieces that matched together would take a long time given the amount of material you had to work with. What if it stumbled across you? Wait, would it even fit? Did you really want to take the chance?

Looking at your supplies again you center in on the lighter. Perhaps if you set fire to a booth away from the Hall? There is a sadistic glee in that thought. After all, didn't everyone look for a reason to set fire to something?

It was passing by again, so you hunker down once more. The spite radiating from the thing is almost suffocating, and you could swear there is a sense of frustration with it. Your need to fight or flee was intensifying, and you knew it would be flight. Only you did not want to run blindly in this abandoned place. There would be no rescue, and you hated to think what would happen when finally faced with the Thing. Thinking rapidly, you decide to set fire to a booth and hope that the Thing is distracted long enough for you to put together a mirror gate. You are not even sure how the mirrors got broken to start with, but you know that in order to help with speed you have to find one with relatively large pieces nearby. If anything, hopefully that will shorten the time you need to puzzle together the exit. You do not know how intelligent the Thing is, but it would be smart not to underestimate it.

The lessening of its presence is a lot like a weight being lifted, and you know it is time. Scrambling to your feet, you cautiously peer over the table to make sure it is not in sight. The faint throb of the ground helps you keep track of its movements, and the haze of its passing can act as your cover as you make your way among the empty booths. Selecting one, you gather trash together to burn.

Your hand shakes as you spin the flint. It takes a few tries, but finally a spark ignites and the small flame flickers forth. Stifling a manic giggle, you touch the flame to the trash and watch it light. You wait until the flame is good and healthy, and then grab a stick or something like it and push the kindling to the corner of one of the wooden booths. The flame sputters as it touches the ice against the wood, and your heart plummets. You had forgotten about that. Thinking rapidly, you look around, and then see the dry area under the table – much like where you have been hiding. Taking your poker, you quickly move the ignited pile to its new location before the cold can extinguish it.

For a few moments you watch the shadows desperately, willing the flame to begin eating at the weakened wood. Everything here was in such a state of neglect, of decay, surely the wood was soft enough for the fire to catch it? Or was it hard wood that caught better? You are not sure, but when you see the smoldering smoke and hear the crackle of flames you cannot help but grin. Just to be sure, you wait until you see the strong glow of the fire and move on to another booth. One would not be enough, you decide. Two in different places, maybe to cause confusion? Mimicking your actions from before, you hear the unmistakable crackle of a burning booth as the new fire is set and realize your time is short. You have to get to the Hall of Mirrors – now!

As you dash in the direction of the Fair's attraction, you feel the rapid thumps of the Thing going to the fire. It is something new in its hunting ground, and it meant to investigate. The stench causes you to stumble, but you keep going. Eventually you climb blindly up the steps to your destination.

Inside, you peer back out to the Fairgrounds. It is out there, the fog intensifying and causing you to see only an outline. It is enough. The thing is too big, and now that you hear its eager breathing you know that if it finds you it does not mean to play. The wickedness dripping from the shadowy form assures you that you do not want to see any details.

As the second booth lights up, you turn indoors and run among the mirrors, trying to find one that is not too damaged. It is not surprising that the ones close to the exit are little more than shells, but closer to the middle, where you entered, there is hope. You hear the Thing howl in anger and stumble towards a set of mirrors that have various large pieces in front of them. Heedless of the slices of pain, you rapidly begin to try and puzzle them together. Testing piece by piece, trying to get them to stick.

The ground shakes as the Thing now quickly moves around the Fairgrounds, the disturbance making it difficult for you to assemble a mirror. A despairing cry escapes you, causing the predator outside to pause. Biting your lip to the point of it bleeding, you quickly continue. Half, just get half put together. You can crawl through!

The building around you shudders as the Thing rams into it.

You scream.

It answers with a hiss.

Working faster now, glass sliding because of the blood but the blood somehow also getting it to stick together because of the intense cold causing it to congeal with preternatural speed, you assemble a third of the large mirror. You can get through if you crawl, but will it work? There are so many cracks; it is not a complete reflection. Granted, it is more than any of the other mirrors, but is it enough?

The next impact causes several of the mirrors nearby to topple and fall.

The urge to flee is too much. Crying, you lower your head and literally plunge into the mirror.

The agony of passage causes you to scream as you crawl along the ground. Unable to take it anymore, you collapse and cry piteously. You are so sure you have failed and will now fall prey to the Thing.

"Hey!" a voice calls as hands carefully touch you.

You scream again as you turn over, looking into the face of a stranger.

He backs up but looks horrified.

You gaze around wildly now.

You see people and working machines, you can smell the collection of aromas, and you can hear the cacophony of sounds, all which are flooding your over-receptive senses. It takes a moment for your panicked brain to realize you are back. You are in pain from all the activity, but it is a welcome sensation.

"Call 911!" your rescuer shouts. "She is covered in cuts!"

Startled at the proclamation, you look at your hands and see that it is true. Not just on the palms and fingertips, where you had been working, but also along the backs. What you can see of your jacket is also shredded, and looking on you see your clothes are in various states of slicing. Reaching up, you are aware that even your face did not escape unscathed. The mirror gate had worked, but due to its damaged state it had shared one last parting gift.

The man who has been talking kneels close and tries to sound encouraging. "It is okay," he says but sounds unsure even to you. "You are going to be okay."

You look at him, still dazed. Your heart is still racing, the pain from wounds within and without is incredible, and you cannot help but wonder what is happening on the other side. Will the Thing try to come through? Can it? For some reason you are certain it cannot. It is too big, and the mirrors there are shattered.

"Really?" you ask the man.

He nods, not sure how else to respond. "Yeah, you will be just fine. Just hang in there, okay? No one is going to hurt you."

You laugh. You cannot help it. You had always heard about hysterical laughter, and now it was bursting from you.

You are not surprised when the man and the surrounding crowd retreats. You are still laughing when the medics arrive. You stop when you get to the hospital, only to find yourself screaming at the sight of any mirror.

No matter what anyone tells you, you are not going to be okay. You know it is there, just beyond the reflective surfaces, waiting.

A Bad Breakup

H.L. Pauff

With your hands on your head, you sat there at the kitchen table, staring blankly at the stove for hours. You hadn't eaten since lunchtime, but you weren't hungry and you had no desire to eat. You had no desire to even move. Life as you knew it was over. The voice of your girlfriend screaming through the phone echoed in your mind.

"I'm breaking up with you! Don't call me anymore!"

Those were words you never thought you'd hear her say. Sure the relationship was only a few months old, but you thought things were going swimmingly well. You'd never been with a woman who shared as many of the same interests as you and you'd never felt so happy to be with someone before.

Sure it was only your second girlfriend, but you thought you had finally found true love. You thought you had found the woman who you would marry and spend the rest of your life with. Apparently, you were wrong and it was the worst feeling in the world. You knew you had screwed it up and your life was over. You would never find love again.

The cold April wind whipped in through the open kitchen window, nipping you in the back of the neck and sending chills through your body. As you stood to shut the window, you noticed how full the moon was and how beautiful and dominating it looked against the night sky. Its bright glow illuminated the street below and your car parked in the driveway glittered. The way your car looked bathed in the moon's light drew a slight grin across your face. It was the as angelic as your old junker would ever look and you knew it was a sign. You grabbed your keys and threw on a coat and rushed down the stairs for a late night drive.

It was freezing in the car and you shivered and your teeth chattered but you were glad to be out of the house. A drive to clear your mind would do you good. You'd figure out a way to win her back.

The car purred to life and you backed out of the driveway. The depth of your seat, the familiar rattling of your engine and the way your breaks squeaked and rumbled made you feel the most comfortable you had felt all day. You couldn't count on women, but you knew you could always count on this car.

You drove through nearly every street in town except for Main Street where the movie theater was located. The last thing you wanted to see were couples holding hands and having fun.

You racked your brain, but no bright ideas on how to win her heart back came to mind. Knowing you had work in the morning, you took the long way home that would lead you through Miller's Hill.

Sitting at the top of the hill, the sight was breathtaking. With the small town lit up and the full moon hanging overhead, it was truly an amazing sight. You wished you had your phone to take a picture.

The brakes squeaked and rumbled as you began the slow descent down the hill. The car seemed to groan more so than usual and the brake pedal wobbled under your foot. The grinding of the brakes grew louder and the wobbling more pronounced until the pedal became loose and went straight to the floor.

Your heart seemed to plummet into your stomach and you felt hollow. Without the brakes to check the car, it slowly began to pick up speed as it rolled down the hill. In a fit of disbelief, you continued to press down on the brake hoping that it would give some measure of resistance, but with every push your foot went straight to the floor.

A million thoughts raced through your head. You thought about opening the door and rolling out, but your runaway car might kill someone. You also thought about jumping into the backseat, but you didn't know how you would explain that to the cops when they found your crashed car.

The car was flying down the hill and headed toward the busy intersection below. You could only see the headlights of the cars crossing, but you knew you couldn't let your car go down there.

You cursed and you screamed and you wailed as you blew through two stop signs at breakneck speed. You were almost at the intersection and you had to do something. As you approached a third stop sign, you grabbed onto the emergency brake and yanked it upwards. The car screeched as it jerked from side to side.

Ten yards away from the intersection, you pulled the wheel to the right, narrowly avoiding a parked car, driving up onto the curb and plowing through someone's fence. As the telephone pole approached, your body went rigid and you closed your eyes.

You didn't hear the violent sounds of the crash, but you felt the airbag exploding in your face and breaking your glasses. The car filled with dust that burned your eyes and nostrils and the hazard lights blinked furiously.

Emerging from the car coughing, you staggered into the street, your heart beating furiously against your chest. Whatever problem or concern plagued your mind earlier seemed so trivial now. You were just glad to be alive.

Short Trip, Long Journey
Jane White

You wake up one morning in the wispy tail of a
dream, a woman laughing, throaty with passion. And
underneath the laugh there is love, oh, there is love. You
reach for her, but she fades away on a regret, and you're
left lying in bed alone. The intimacy of the dream lingers
and warms you, and it's a god-awful wonderful feeling you
didn't know you were missing until this moment.

Maybe you are done with self-pity. Maybe you
throw caution to the winds, and sign up for an online
dating service. You build your profile carefully; you don't
want to scare anyone off. You leave out more than you put
in. You know it's stupid, you know this can only end in
disaster, but what have you got to lose, really? Nothing,
that's what.

In the next couple of weeks you review the matches
you've been sent. You try to stay detached, tell yourself
this is just an intellectual exercise, you'll never meet these
women. But you can't help but feel a tiny frisson of
excitement, because what if? What if what? You don't
know what, but there is possibility. And it's been a long,
long time since there has been any possibility in your life.

You decide to call three of them. You agonize whether you should be honest, and you decide what the hell. You are honest with the first woman, and her laugh has a car crash quality that tells you everything about her, and you hang up without even continuing the conversation. You decide to try a different tack with the second. You come off as evasive, and she politely tells you she is only interested in open, honest relationships and hangs up.

You wonder if you should even try number three. But maybe, just maybe you sensed something about this one, and you were unconsciously saving the best for last. Yeah, that's it, you tell yourself. One more. You pat the dog to remind yourself you still have a friend, no matter what. He licks your hand.

You call the third woman. Her name is Amy, and you hit it off right away. Before you realize it, you've been talking for an hour. You tell her all the wonderful places you've traveled, and that you play the violin. She tells you she plays the harp, and you discover you share a love of cheesy show tunes. You find out she loves peanut butter and pickle sandwiches and bad reality TV, and that she hates dolls. She tells you it is a common fear called Pediophobia. She has a high, musical laugh that Herman must be able to hear through the phone, because it makes his tail thump against the floor. You ask her if she likes dogs and she says yes, she loves animals, why, do you have dog? You hesitate. All you say is yes, I do. His name is Herman. She asks if you want to meet. You're so thrown off by this you immediately answer yes, because yes, you want desperately to meet her, this girl who loves animals and is afraid of dolls. You want to share a peanut butter and pickle sandwich with her and lick the juice from her fingers, and maybe peanut butter form the corner of her mouth. You are immediately appalled by this thought, and you know you will fantasize about it later.

You arrange to meet at a coffee shop downtown. She says she will recognize you from you profile picture. Your heart sinks, because it is an old picture, which is kind of like cheating. OK, you say. You don't tell her you will recognize her too.

After you get off the phone, you realize the futility of all of this, and you begin wading back into the pity pond, the scummy pond of self-doubt and loathing. You get about half way, and then you stop. What if? You ask yourself. What's the worst that can happen? You know she will be polite enough to at least have a cup of coffee with you. You decide to go for it.

The day before your date, you sleep fitfully. But you wake up energized, because this is the biggest thing, the biggest challenge you've taken on in quite a while. It sings in your veins. You remind yourself to remember that no matter what happens, how good it feels to try. You take extra time with your grooming and dress carefully. You ask Herman how you look. His tail thumps against the kitchen chair in a steady rhythm, and you take that as a lookin' good, buddy.

You slap on some cologne, but the chemical smell is so overwhelming, you wash it off. You tell yourself to quit stalling, and you put on your coat. Herman follows you to the door. Not this time buddy, you tell him. This time I'm flyin' solo.

You make your way to the bus stop. You sit on the bench and pretend you are just enjoying the day, the sun on your face. Maybe you won't get on the bus. Maybe you will just sit here for a while, then go home and take Herman for a walk. You hear the bus coming long before it gets to the stop. The air breaks hiss and the doors squeak open.

You get on the bus and find your seat. Luckily this time of day the bus isn't crowded. You feel relieved to be on the bus, and as it pulls away from the bus stop, you are lulled by the ocking motion. You ponder the complex mix of scents in the stale air filled with the breath and life of your fellow commuters; baby powder and soiled diapers, coffee, gum, last night's alcohol overlaid with too much cologne or perfume. You wonder if Amy will be wearing perfume. You hope not. You imagine she looks like your 6th grade teacher, Mrs. Griffith. Soft curly hair, kind eyes, and a juicy plumpness that you want to sink into. And god, you hope she wears the same fuzzy cardigan sweaters with the top two buttons undone, that show the little hollow at the base of her throat. You think about peanut butter and pickle sandwiches.

The bus driver calls out your stop. You almost don't get off. Just the fantasy of meeting Amy has been worth it. Why ruin it? But you decide what the hell, might as well get a cup of coffee. Your heart is racing, your legs trembling as you step carefully from the bus. You're trembling so hard, you trip on the last step, and fly off the bus flailing like a jerky marionette. Someone asks if you're OK. You nod, burning with shame. Looking around is futile because you know you won't see her, that she probably turned and bolted down an alley as soon as she saw you. You start to walk because you just want to get away, away from your stupid self and all the people who you know are looking at you. You chastise yourself for not bringing Herman. Why, oh why, didn't you bring Herman? Then you hear your name. You stop, because you're not sure you really heard it. George, she says again. You made it. I'm so glad. She hugs you and she smells mouth-watering, like warm bread and butter. She takes your arm, the one not holding the white cane. She asks why you didn't bring Herman. And that's when you know everything is going to be okay.

The Spectrum of Precipitation

Jeff Moscaritolo

You don't know her at all. Her name is Audrey –
you know that much. But you had never even seen her
until a few days ago, when she came up to you in the
student union teeming with undergraduates who are
plenty more attractive than you, many of whom you've
reluctantly taught these last two years while you chip away
at your likely-to-be-obsolete master's degree. And she,
Audrey, asked you out of nowhere if you'd like to go to a
poetry reading, and what else were you supposed to do?
Yes, she was cute, and yes, you snuck a glance at her chest.
Maybe the invite was a little unexpected, and maybe all
that bohemian stuff isn't really your thing, but let's be
frank: you're no longer at a stage in your life in which you
should be turning women down.

So...a poetry reading. How bad could it be?

You pick Audrey up at her apartment and drive
through the slowly falling mist of the early evening.
"Mizzle," she says once she's in the car. No hello. Just
launching right into conversation.

"What's that?" you say.

"The name for this kind of weather. Mizzle. Not as foggy as mist, but not as heavy as drizzle. It's all part of a spectrum, see."

"Did you make that up?"

"The spectrum?"

"The word. Mizzle."

She laughs. This was a funny thing for you to say. "I think maybe Jane Austen coined the term," she says. "In one of her books. Or, at least, she certainly uses it in one of them. I forget which one. Maybe Pride, but I'm not sure. But yeah. Jane Austen. That's where I learned it."

You take note of the way she uses the present tense when talking about literature in casual conversation. Life is an English paper to her. "I didn't know that," you say.

She smiles at you through her angular black frames. "Yeah, Jane Austen is my boo," she says. "Isn't it a great word though? It's just so spot-on. Mizzle. It's like, when I say it, I can feel the droplets of water on my face, like little pin-pricks or something. It's like walking outside when it's mizzling – it gives you that tingling feeling on your skin, and it's almost as though your whole body is experiencing blood loss. Like if you cross your legs for too long, but with your whole body." She sighs to herself. "Your whole body is asleep. Such is life," she says.

You start to tune her out. Is she always saying weird things like this, talking about words she likes? Or is it just because she's around you – maybe she gets validation from sounding smart to you, a non-literature type. She doesn't anticipate that maybe you know a thing or two of art and of postmodernism – you try to recall a lecture, back in college. An art history class. Or maybe it was communication theory. Or even just a few snippets of knowledge left over from conversations with Katie, conversations that have since faded and become nothing more than a vague arrangement of discarded emotions somewhere in your brain. Whichever, you learned all about this sort of thing, how language is just a construct and how words only carry meaning if we assign them meaning. But you don't say anything about this out loud. You don't want a discussion about it. You hit the windshield wiper once. It screeches along the glass like an upset child.

She navigates to the coffee shop, a grimy-looking brick rectangle of a building, a garage-style door on the side with establishment's name spray-painted on it in purple – The Local Mocha. You probably wouldn't have even known it was there if you passed it on your own. The gravel crunches as you pull into a space next to a sedan covered hood-to-trunk in bumper stickers. Peace sign stickers, Coexist stickers, green technology, gay rights, vegan diets. One sticker just beneath the handle on the driver's side door says in all capital letters: WE'RE LIBERAL: WE LIBERATE.

The weather has cleared up. As you get out of the car, Audrey ties her hair to the side in a loose ponytail and says, "Did you know that if you Google 'anagram,' it asks you if you mean 'nag a ram?'"

"Me specifically?" you say.

"Anyone. Not just you," she says, and then adds, "Google is pretty nonbiased."

"No kidding."

"Nag a ram," she says again. "It's an anagram of 'anagram.' Isn't that clever?"

"Oh I see."

She nods, puts a cigarette to her lips, lights it. She takes a big drag and puffs it out in a single quick burst of smoke. "Fucking meta, right?"

"Indeed," you say, letting your elbow brush against hers. "Sorry, I just forgot what an anagram was. I get it confused with acronym sometimes."

"Most people do," she says.

You wonder about this, about her perception of most people. You wonder where her perception of herself fits into this perception. Fucking meta, you think.

"So," she says, "where do you think you are on the spectrum of precipitation?"

"What?"

She kicks at a particularly large piece of gravel in the road. "It's just a getting-to-know-you question. If you were a kind of precipitation, what kind would you be?"

"I don't know," you say.

"Not mizzle?"

"I'd have to think about it."

"I would be rain. A light shower maybe. Nothing like a torrential downpour or anything. But just enough rain to make other ambient noise dissolve within me."

You wonder how long you can keep this up. You remind yourself that, hey, you can always sleep with her tonight and never speak to her again, and then you won't have to bother remembering this conversation. You know you shouldn't, but you think of Katie, of the rainy night last year when she came home from work at the Adams Street Grille and ended the engagement, just like that. So yes, maybe you are going to this reading just to get into this girl's pants, but really what's wrong with that? Who wouldn't withstand a less than enjoyable social situation in exchange for a little company?

Audrey says, "So? What you would be?"

"Acid rain," you say. "Searing, burning acid rain." She stops walking a moment, looks at you in silence, then laughs and swats your arm.

A circle of maybe six people stand outside The Local Mocha, a few of them smoking cigarettes. They stand with their hands in their pockets. Corduroy pants. T-shirts displaying the names of obscure bands. Wrinkly plaid flannels. Hair that sweeps down and to the side. Beards everywhere. One young man, a red-head, wears a loose-fitting San Fransisco 49ers jersey, and the other members of the group mock him for this. Audrey introduces you. Everyone waves in unison, looking at you like you don't really matter in the grand scheme of things.

You take note of one young woman, a tall girl with long limbs. A complicated series of tattoos spiral down her left arm – branches, flames, a multicolored snake – the pattern reaching all the way down to the point between her index and middle finger so that she appears to be wearing a lace glove, and on the other arm the sentence, No one has power over me, is written in a sloppy yet somehow beautiful font that you assume is her own handwriting. Her hair, glossy black with pink tips, is tossed haphazardly over to one side of her head, and she wears a long black open cardigan that seems to float in the autumn breeze. She doesn't have a purse, just a small backpack with metal buttons pinned to the straps. You take note of her hips, the way they're cocked to the side, unintentionally seductive. Or maybe it's entirely intentional and you just don't know it.

People migrate indoors. Audrey hooks her arm in yours and tugs you into the coffee shop, through the main beverage area to the back room, an art studio with hard cement floors. A few artists sit working at wooden tables wearing ratty clothing stained with flecks of dried paint. They look up from their masterpieces-to-be at the group ambling through the studio and around to the room on the far side of the building, the performance space.

A small black wooden stage occupies the back half – or is it the front half – of the room, jutting up against the inside of the garage-style door. Painted across the garage door in big letters is a message: FUKC THE POWERS THAT BEE. You don't know why the last two letters in "fuck" are switched or why "be" is spelled like the insect, but you assume it must have significance for somebody somewhere. The space is dimly lit, the walls painted in dark purple hues, the floor gray and barren. A few oscillating fans have been positioned on the sides of the room, adding a mechanical buzz to the ambience of the place. Folding chairs face the stage where a microphone has been positioned next to a music stand. Audrey directs you to a pair of mismatched chairs in the back row.

The room starts to fill up. Some people have brought pillows from home to drop on the floor and sit on. A young man with a pointy goatee and a Raiders cap sits next to you and strikes up conversation with Audrey. She leans in, places her hand on your thigh while she chit-chats, and you sit in between and stay quiet, smiling.

Eventually a young woman with a big paisley scarf coiled over her shoulders approaches the microphone and the audience gets quiet. She thanks everyone for coming and encourages everyone to support The Local Mocha and buy lots of coffee and smoothies and muffins, because, and let's be honest here, guys, they don't have to let us use this space for these readings and we all should appreciate the blessing that The Local Mocha has given us all. And then she calls up the first reader, some guy named Chase – let's give it up for Chase – who you recognize from the ring of smokers outside. He wears a pair of tight knee-high shorts and a golfer's cap.

You find it difficult to keep your eyes focused on this young man as he reads. He presses his mouth close to the microphone and speaks into it, an amplified near-whisper. He seems to force his voice into a lilting melody, rolling up in pitch and then back down. You let your eyes wander around the room, up toward the ceiling, think, people don't talk like this, all sing-songy. There is something self-aggrandizing about the way he tries to make the poetry sound like poetry. At some point you hear him say the word "testicle," loud and over-enunciated, the consonants popping in the microphone.

You resist the urge to pull your phone from your pocket and check the time.

Chase finishes his reading, a round of hushed applause, and then up comes the next reader, a pale young man in a pinstripe jacket and a bright purple t-shirt with the word PRIDE in rainbow lettering. You decide he will read poems about gay people. Most likely, he will use words like "bitch" and "girlfriend" and "this lady," referring to himself in ironic and sassy ways. You cross your hands in your lap and let your eyes wander over the backs of people's heads. You think about the textures of their hairstyles.

More people get up to read, one by one, and you let the poetry wash over you. You silently admit that you are finding the experience relaxing. You aren't bored or sleepy – you're just letting yourself dissolve into the atmosphere, like a drop of ink into the ocean. Before you know it, five readers have come and gone. The announcer woman, the self-proclaimed master of ceremonies in the paisley scarf, returns to the microphone and utters the words "last but not least," and you're relieved to know that the night is almost done. You sneak a glance at Audrey in the dim light and smile at her.

"You're having fun?" she whispers.

You nod. "Yeah, it's great."

And then the final speaker for the evening steps up to the stage – the girl with the tattoo sleeve and the messy hair and the hips. You feel yourself slide forward in your seat. Audrey pats your thigh. "Don't worry," she says. "After Nadine is done we'll get out of here and do something that's more like what you would want to do."

"Sure," you say quietly, and immediately afterward you wish you had said something that sounded more excited, but before you can, Nadine starts into her reading, and you don't want to be rude.

"So, this piece," she says, and the deepness of her voice surprises you, a rich yet feminine baritone, commanding. She stands like she did earlier, hip thrust out. "Yeah, so, I just composed a draft of this a couple days ago. So it's still pretty rough." She swipes a hand through her hair, scrunches up a fistful of it, lets it drop. "Sorry," she says, and you notice that the hand holding the journal is shaking slightly. "Microphones. They just, I don't know, they just make me feel uncomfortable." She taps the head of the microphone. "I mean, look at this thing. Just right here in my face. It's, like, the most annoying kind of penis."

Someone in the audience yells, "You'll do great, Nadine!"

She holds up a fist, "Thanks, friend," she says. The audience chuckles and she shakes her head out – you like the way the pink tips of her hair fan out around her like wild feathers. You find her bashfulness endearing, and then you wonder if she planned to be bashful. "Okay, here goes," she says.

And then her poem begins like a jackhammer, a quick series of staccato words that seem to punch their way out of the speakers at the edges of the stage. She starts with nouns, all external body parts.

Skin. Nostril. Fingers. Hips.

She rattles them off quickly, enunciating with a heightened crispness.

Pores. Lips. Taste buds. Hair follicles. Abdomen. Nipples.

You notice that she's started in on the female anatomy. Sexualized body parts.

Breasts. Vagina. Clitoris.

There's a quiet anger to the way she's saying these words, and you can't help thinking... it's kind of hot. You let your eyes scan her up and down. You imagine her completely nude, her clothes rumpled on the floor behind her, a bright spotlight shining on her slender body. You picture the subtle slope of her breasts, the slight crease tracing down the middle of her stomach. Her navel. And then, bam, she says Navel and you feel utterly connected.

Fallopian tube. Eye socket. Aorta. Heart.

You become suddenly aware of Audrey at your elbow, and you wonder how obvious you are. Do the impure thoughts in your head show on your face? You keep your eyes forward and focus on Nadine's words.

Gripping me. Hands gripping me. Lips. Your eyes on me. Every part of me. A hand springing from your chest and reaching into mine.

You're not even really sure what this poem is about. Something sexual. You're fairly certain it's something sexual. Or certainly, you want it to be sexual, and then you're back in your reverie, picturing Nadine's tattooed hand rubbing your bare chest, her body swaying above yours. Her poem quickens, her voice deepening. She leans in closer to the microphone, getting louder.

Too hard. Lips. Cheek. Nose. Eyelashes. Control.

She looks up at the audience every few words.

Your strength over me. Physical strength. Forcing surrender.

Her voice becoming angrier now. She looks up quickly, makes eye contact with you, just for an instant, a flicker of a moment.

I surrender. Scream. Surrender. Scream. Surrender.

She looks up again, her eyes linger on yours, and you feel your stomach lifting, as if it has been pumped full of air, a feeling you remember from times past, the feeling of being on the verge of something. When your mother discovered your stash of weed in your room. The late night phone call from your father that you knew would be the news of your grandmother's death. Seeing the expression on Katie's face that told you this wasn't just a normal fight, that this was the real thing.

Earlobes. Wrists. No more surrender.

You divert your eyes and look down at your shoes, the legs crossed at the ankles. They feel like someone else's ankles.

Forehead. Temple. I'm done. Ribcage. Tongue. Done with surrender.

You cross your legs, uncross them, cross them again. You don't know what to do with your hands so you fold them in your lap.

Fingers. Lips. And if you bite. Torso. Hips. I will bite back.

Nadine gives a quick nod and bends down to grab her bottle of water from the floor next to her. The applause erupts from the audience, a rush of noise. You clap along with them. You clap and clap. Nadine nods again, closes her notebook, and walks off the stage quickly, swallowed and absorbed into the crowd of anonymous writers.

You're silent most of the drive. You keep thinking of Nadine, her slender face, glossy hair, her tattoos. Surely she had other tattoos in places you couldn't see.

Outside the night sky is big and clear, the stars crisp. The moon glows bright and silver, its light falling over the brick buildings like a sheet.

Audrey looks at you. "So?"

"Yes?"

"What did you think?"

"I enjoyed it."

"Yeah? You liked it? You liked the reading? You're not just being polite."

"Well, yes I suppose I am being polite," you say, and then you look at her. You make sure to establish eye contact. "But I also enjoyed it."

"Truth?" she says.

"Yes," you say, and then you add, "Honest and polite aren't exclusive."

"Hey now," she says. "That was pretty deep."

She places her hand over yours where it rests on the manual shift.

You pull into her apartment complex and find a space right out front. You yank up the parking brake, but you keep the car running. "Well," she says, and she smiles at you. You glance at the clock above the radio. It's early yet. "You coming up for a bit?"

You let your jaw hover open to make it look like you need to consider this. "I don't know," you say. "Are you going to drug me and chain me to the bed and steal my things?"

She laughs. "I hadn't planned on that," she says.

You reach for the keys. "Well I guess it's safe then."

Inside, she tells you to make yourself comfortable and continues straight on down a short hallway to what you assume is her bedroom. The living room is dimly lit. The wall on the far side of the room, near the kitchen, is decorated floor-to-ceiling with hand-scratched writing. You squint in the dim light at the wall but can't make out any words, the cursive too complex and small, and you decide not to bother getting a better look. It's a poem of some sort, you can assume that much, but you've had enough poetry for one evening. And it probably is just decorative anyway. You sit on the wide leather couch and swing your shoes up onto the coffee table, then on second thought you drop you feet back down to the floor.

Audrey returns with a small metal canister in the shape of a jelly bean. She sits next to you and opens the canister, dropping the lid on the table. She pulls out a plastic bag, tied off at the end, and a glass pipe shaped like a panda, the bowl hollowed into the panda's stomach.

"Oh," you say. "So we're smoking then?"

She looks up from the canister, then back down at it. She closes her eyes and inhales sharply. "Oh gosh, that's embarrassing. I'm sorry I just – I just assumed."

"No, no it's cool."

"Wow. That was really rude of me. Um..." she pauses there in front of you, not knowing whether to put the stuff away or to keep it out. "I didn't even ask if you –"

"It's fine, Audrey. Really."

"I just thought it would be fun."

You consider whether her embarrassment is genuine. This could be her thing, her very own social-maneuvering technique – asking a person to do something by thinking she already asked. Or perhaps she honestly feels embarrassed and you're simply reading too much into it.

You lean in and give her a quick kiss, and when you pull away she's smiling. Apparently a kiss was the right thing to do. "It'll be fun," you say.

She picks apart a chunk of marijuana and fills the panda. She hands the pipe and lighter to you. "So who did you like best?" she says.

"Who?"

"Tonight. The poets. Who did you like best?"

"Well," and then you light the bowl, letting the panda's bloated tummy fill with milky white smoke before taking it in. "I mean, it's not really my thing, you know, so it's hard for me to say who was best," you say, passing the panda back to her.

"You're not going to be graded," she says.

"Well," you say. "That last girl. Woman. The last woman, she was pretty good."

"Oh yeah," she says. She hits the bowl and passes it back to you. "Yeah, Nadine is badass."

You nod and take another hit. "Yes she is," you say. You rub your palms together. You stretch the fingers out, open, closed, open. You're feeling the tingling sensation sliding down your limbs and creeping over the back of your head like a hand, seizing hold of you. And now she's already handing the thing back to you, and you're hitting it again, coughing a little.

You say, "So you guys have these things pretty often?"

"The readings?"

"Yeah."

"What, do you want to go to another?"

"I don't mean to say – I don't know, I was just asking." When she remains silent you add, "Sure. If you want. That could be fun, sure."

She looks out the sides of her eyes. "Maybe."

"Or not. That's fine too. Either one is fine."

"I'm sorry. I mean, you're a nice guy and all. I just don't want us getting ahead of ourselves here."

"Who is getting ahead?" you say.

She looks down, flicks the lighter near the bowl. "I think it's done," she says. She looks back at you, eyes narrow, just slits in her face where the light can get out. "What is the goal of tonight?" she says.

"Is this another getting-to-know you question?"

"I mean what are you looking for? What are you hoping will come of this?"

You start shaking your head. "I don't know. I'm just – I don't know."

"Sorry, I just want to be clear with you. Because beyond tonight I'm not really looking for much."

"Okay," you say, and you know it shouldn't hurt you to hear this but it does, the idea that you are not desired. Or at least not in the way you may have thought.

"Okay?" she says.

"Yeah," you say. "Okay."

Audrey smiles. She slides closer to you on the couch and her leg touches yours, and you wonder about the name Audrey. You wonder which name came first,

Audrey or Aubrey. If someone came up with the original name, and then the variation happened by mistake. Somebody forgetting in the heat of the baby-naming moment which direction the letter b faced. As your lips caress hers and your hands glide over her body, underneath her clothing, her skin, you consider this concept – one name existing as a mutation of another. One person existing as the mutation of another person.

After letting yourself doze for a few hours, you rise slowly and sweep your leg along the floor next to her bed until you locate your pile of clothes. Outside the wind has picked up a little, shuddering against side of the building like a whisper. Your eyes adjust themselves as you dress, and she rolls onto her stomach, exposing the bare curve of her back to the darkness. Her eyes flicker open. She looks up at you, still not quite awake, and says in a groggy voice, "What time is it?"

"I don't know, but it's getting breezy out."

Her eyes slide closed and her lips curl into a lopsided smile. "You know, you're pretty good at that."

"At what?"

"Saying things like that." She exhales deeply and slips back into sleep.

You enter your apartment and drop your keys on the counter. You saunter into your room, pull a damp bath towel off the bed – it must have been collected there in a pile since this morning – and you let it fall to the floor. You sit at the edge of the bed and glance at the dresser, on top of which stands an ornate glass bottle, nearly emptied of its liquid. It is a bottle of Katie's perfume – some French name you don't know how to pronounce. Not that it would matter if you did. She left the bottle at your place when she moved out a year ago. You found it in the bathroom, moved it to the dresser. Back then, you reminded her multiple times that the bottle was still there, waiting for her to come get it, but she never did. A bottle like that, nearly empty, it just wasn't worth having to see you again. And then time passed, and you kept intending to get rid of it, but you never did, and now here you are, sitting on your bed and staring at the thing.

Second Nature

Judy Klass

The yellow school bus rolls up in slow motion and groans to a stop. The doors sigh open and you climb aboard. You nod to Rodney, the driver, but he does not acknowledge you; he lives in a sealed, abstracted world. Still, you would like to sit up front, in a seat near him, for the flimsy sense of protection that a seat near a grown-up can give you. But Charlene, a fifth grader, is carrying a tuna fish sandwich for lunch in a paper bag and the smell of it makes you feel ill (a lot of smells on the bus and in school make you feel ill), so you have no choice but to head toward the back.

You find an empty seat and stare out the dirty window. Suburbia spackled and smeared with a muddy film. Not five minutes have gone by when Mark Policastro and Donny Whitewood start to mess with you. They are high school kids, a few years older than you are, but somehow it makes them feel tough to bully a girl like you. They rise from the seat on which they have lounged, and both of them lean over yours, staring down at you and smirking. "Hey, Cresskill," Mark says. "You got a new mommy and daddy this month?"

You stare straight ahead.

"Cresskill, look at me when I'm talking to you, bitch!" Mark says, and kicks your leg, hard. Ow.

You look at him. A big, hulking Cro-Magnon, already pushing six feet tall, in ninth grade. He's not supposed to be standing up on the bus, blocking the aisle. His voice is loud enough that it must carry to the front, but both you and he know that Rodney won't tell him to get back in his seat. Rodney tunes out all this stuff.

"I live with my grandmother," you tell Mark.

"Yeah, only because they can't find a foster home that wants your reject ass," Mark sneers. "Maybe if you weren't such a dog and a freakazoid weirdo, you could have an actual family."

"Maybe." You give him a big, fake, warm smile. The emotions coming off of him are easy to read. Bullies have their own way of thinking about things. Cruelty and intimidation light up their central nervous systems in bright, happy colors.

"Don't look at me that way, bitch!" he says, and slaps at your hair and the side of your head. The barrette on one side digs into your scalp. "Don't look at me at all. Ever."

You look away. He lazily browses through his mind for new ways to mess with you. But at this point, Donny nudges him. "Look at the fairy," Donny whispers, and they both focus their attention on Gary Hamlisch, two seats back.

"That goes double for you, you little faggot!" Mark explodes, and he and his sidekick drift back to stand over Gary's seat. "If I ever catch you looking at me, I will break both your hands off and shove them up your faggotty asshole. Would you enjoy that, Gary? Would you get off on that?"

They zero in on Gary, exclusively. You are off the hook for the rest of the ride. Gary's a nice guy; it was incautious of him to be caught staring during the bullying.

You and Gary cannot save each other, and so you are better off ignoring each other's misery.

*

At last the bus pulls into the parking lot. You and the rest of the middle school kids head to the left, and the high school kids head toward their building on the right. You hate this place. But you will have to keep coming back here, every day, for a long, long time.

In home room, Mr. Bassett drones at the class about socio-economic challenges in Africa and Latin America, and you tune out. Social studies can be exciting, if people open themselves up and feel what people in different societies, different situations, might be feeling. Mr. Bassett has no such capacity. For him, the old accepted wisdom of Modernization Theory is enough; third world countries must learn from the US and copy the US, and then they will be like us. He heard that theory disparaged by his own teachers in college, but to him it still feels right. You can sense, when the textbook warns against ethnocentrism and discusses years of exploitation, how the words bounce harmlessly off the man's inner core of belief.

You make it through math. You make it through Spanish class. There is something appealing about the way Mrs. Murillo thinks in Spanish; it diverts you and aids your comprehension. But it's disturbing to sit next to Oliver Davenport. He's so quiet; he gets through school pretty much unobserved. You wonder if anyone besides you knows he is a sociopath.

You are sitting by yourself at the long lunchroom table, eating the lettuce, tomato and cheese sandwich you brought because you can't handle cafeteria food. You get a kind of buzz off of the dizzy thoughts and mood swings flying through Sheryl Sullivan's head. You can't catch the thoughts, exactly – you rarely can. But her emotions keep shifting, changing like the color of a mood ring, as she thinks of her favorite reality show, and then of how the boy she has a crush on ignored her in homeroom, and then of how it will feel to be in high school and buy a low-cut prom dress. You're almost drunk on this flood of sensations washing through her, cresting and crashing like waves.

Gary pulls you out of that ocean, as he plunks his tray down next to you and sits. You're not sure this is a good idea, but you give him a smile. "Hey," you say.

"Hey, yourself." He starts to eat. "So, Lily," he says at last. "What are we going to do about this Mark Policastro situation?"

You shrug. "Nothing we can do. Rodney won't help, the school won't help."

"It has to stop. There's no way he can keep doing that."

You are silent. There is nothing to say.

"I told my dad," he says. "He told me to tough it out, stand up to him. I'm like, Dad, I'm a seventh grader, we're talking about a couple of ninth graders . . . He won't help. What about your grandma?"

You look down at your sandwich. "She just tells me that school is like this. Life is like this. It's always going to be this way."

"That's no kind of answer!"

You can't give him a different one. Gary isn't even out to himself yet, but you've known for several years that he is gay. He's wondering, now, whether to acquire you as a girlfriend; would that rain down more teasing on both your heads, or less? You're not sure yourself. His emotions toward you are mixed. He's basically a decent fellow and feels a kind of indignation at a girl getting bullied that's old-fashioned and chivalrous. No other guy on the school bus feels that way about it. Yet he is frustrated by his inability to be attracted to you, or any girl.

In your case, he wonders whether your refusal to dress nicely, with proper hair and makeup, is to blame.

"The way I see it," you tell him at last, "is that we just have to do our time here, and then get out. And whatever we run into, out there – it won't be as bad. And if it is, we get to leave."

*

After lunch is science class. You do not want to dissect a fetal pig. But the day is coming soon. This class is just prep work for that kind of lab work.

And then there is gym class. Thank God, it is not one of the coed days. You don't really mind the sneering, appraising attitude of the other girls in the locker room and on the court. You are the last one picked for a basketball team, but that's all right. Sheryl is here, not dizzy and lost in a world of her own as she was during lunch. Now she is part of the collective, and you are outside of it. But it is a snippy collective, not a menacing one. There are girls out there with the same coiled snarl of aggressive meanness inside of them as can be found in a Mark Policastro, but there are none of them in your gym class, this term. Cattiness and condescension are much easier to metabolize – an environment in which you can swim along perfectly well.

English is your last class of the day. Miss Clark means so well. She beams at you, as always. You find it oppressive. She goes around the room handing back papers, and softly whispers as she gives you yours, "Please stay after class, Lily, and talk with me for a while." Uh oh. You nod.

After class, she's ready to bond with you, and get close to you. Her every thought, word and gesture is drenched in emotion. What you get off of her is a subtle kind of smugness, a terribly righteous sense of how sensitive she is, how willing to reach out to troubled children in need. You'd like to tell her to blow it out her ear.

"Lily," she says to you, after the others are gone. "I'd like to know why you always write your autobiographical essays in second person. You know what second person is, don't you?"

"Yes, ma'am."

"Most people use first-person narration when they write. It seems that you never do."

She waits, for you to reveal some big answer to her. You shrug.

"Don't get me wrong – you're a wonderful writer! With a touch of the poet about you – some lines of your paper . . . It doesn't sound like a seventh grader at all. You're an old soul. But you spend so much time in your essays talking about what other people are thinking and feeling. And yes, it's remarkable how you try to see through their eyes! But what about what you feel?"

Again, you shrug. "I guess I'm just experimenting. Or – whatever," you mumble, at last.

"The reason I ask about second person," she says softly, thrilling herself with her own self-perceived empathy, "is that sometimes, when people find their situation painful, they revert to the second person. There were twin boys in Canada, for example, and there was an accident when one was circumcised – and the doctors turned him into a girl, and his family raised him as a girl. But he never felt like a girl, and eventually, he had himself turned back into a man. When he talks about himself – what it was like for him growing up the way he did – he says 'you.' You feel that something isn't right. You know your parents mean well, but you can't talk to them about your feelings. That kind of thing."

Miss Clark stares at you intently as she talks. You give her a bland smile. You blink at her.

"People with PTSD also sometimes talk about themselves, about their combat experiences, about what it's like to be home, in the second person," she goes on. "And so I just wonder – is there something really painful, something that you're distancing yourself from, when you write this way?"

You sure wish you could distance yourself from her right now. Her eagerness to uncover some adolescent misery, some sexual secret, some private horror, is so palpable, it makes it hard for you to breathe. You get a whiff of a hope, on her part, that you are a victim of abuse. She smothers you with her concern – she wants to revel in your pain.

"I'll try to use first person in the future," you say.

"But that's not my point."

"I was just experimenting, ma'am. I'll write normal essays from now on." You gather your books and the paper she's handed back, signaling that you're ready to go. She backs off a little bit. For the heck of it, as you stand, you throw her a bone. "In terms of stuff bugging me – on the school bus, Mark Policastro and Donny Whitewood give me a hard time. Me and Gary Hamlisch. They're ninth graders and we're both seventh graders –"

"And they're bullying you?"

"Yes, ma'am. Some days."

She presses your arm warmly. "I'm so glad you told me, Lily. I'll look into it," she promises.

Maybe she will and maybe she won't. Maybe she can convince indifferent school administrators to act, as they never have before. Maybe she'll raise a ruckus that will only lead to more bullying, to you getting the crap beaten out of you, as has happened in years gone by. Or, maybe she'll earnestly pass along the information and it will plink harmlessly off the ears of the principal and vice principal as it usually does, never remotely affecting the course of events.

*

You're not sorry to have missed the school bus home. You take a public city bus. You get off eight blocks from your house, where there is a little strip mall. You buy a pack of sugarless gum in the candy store, and linger by the counter. You're fascinated by the pattern of perception in the mind of the middle-aged Korean man who runs this store, who is in it from early in the morning until late at night. You could not come close to reading thoughts in Korean. But you get sensations of homesickness, a sense of his self-discipline, his hopes for his children, his anxieties about a son who does not study hard enough . . . There is something touching and wondrously alien about his mind, and something appealing about his aching nostalgia for a village in the mountains. You can almost see the contours of it, blurred by snow.

You dawdle as you walk homeward. It is 5:30 when you unlock the door of your grandmother's one-story house. You are dismayed to find your older half-brother Kevin inside, waiting for you.

"Lily," he says.

"Hey," you tell him.

Kevin's a grown man, and he's got a desk job working for the Department of Sanitation. He's very proud of that job. You can barely remember when you were small, and he and you and your mom were all rattling around in the same apartment.

"I came by to see Grandma," he says. "And I thought I'd stick around until you got home. How are you?"

"Good, good. Everything's good."

"Are you making friends in school?"

"Sure. Lots."

"You know I'd ask you to come live with me, Lily, if I was in that kind of situation. But I'm at work all the time, I live far from the school and it's just a little studio apartment – "

"It's fine, Kevin. I'm doing fine with Grandma."

Talking to him is a little like talking to Miss Clark, though he's not one to gush. You can sense him congratulating himself for taking an interest in you. But it's a hard shell he's put around himself, in a vain, life-long attempt to ward off empathic probing such as you are capable of – and perhaps to thwart any abilities he himself might have along those lines. Perhaps he caught a surge of some strong feeling, somewhere along the line, and it freaked him out – and he won't risk it happening again. He takes grim satisfaction in the way he has disengaged. You can catch glimpses of the other emotions that have always been there with him: the deep-seated secret conviction of certain first-born children that there was no need for any more after him – his birth is where the family should have stopped. And the anger borne of his years living with Mom: frustration and roiling pain, directed toward her, for her carelessness and callousness and eventual madness, borne of sensitivity. Rage at her for being drugged-out, and then for being gone. All projected onto you now, a legacy of suppressed fury, since you look a bit like her.

Does he really think he has you fooled? Does he, of all people, not understand how well you've been reading him since you were small?

"Well, any time you feel a need for a talk with your big brother, you give me a call. You got my cell phone number?"

"Sure, Kevin. I got it."

"Good." He tousles your hair awkwardly, causing it to frizz and wisp out of the barrettes. And then he is gone.

You knock on your grandmother's bedroom door.

"Come in," she says.

You enter her small, neat room. You like living with Grandma. This is the most restful part of the day.

"We got chicken in the house? For dinner?" she asks.

"No, Grandma. But I can run to the corner store."

"That's a good girl. There are two five-dollar bills in my purse. Maybe get some tomatoes to cook with it." She closes her eyes.

Grandma was a pleasant surprise to you, when you finally met her when you were ten. A daughter howling with pain and self-pity, acting out and screaming at her, stealing money for drugs, had caused Grandma to withdraw into herself; you had been through two foster homes by the time you found out she was alive. After you did your time in one more disastrous foster home, she decided she liked you enough to take you in.

You don't talk to her directly about your abilities. About feeling like a raw nerve, constantly being poked at. About fleeting moments of voyeuristic wonder, and joy. You can feel that she never fully understood it when Mom talked to her about it, while growing up. She doesn't want to hear it again, or try to understand it. She's just tired.

But she gets that you're different from most people. She gets that you don't make as big a fuss about it as her daughter did, and she's grateful. She tells you to keep your head down and muddle through, and it's not bad advice. Don't feel things too deeply. Just try to observe people. People are interesting.

You close the bedroom door softly. You get the two fives from her purse, and head out toward the corner store.

Stark, Dead Alone

Layla Layton

You own nothing. This is how you justify it to yourself as you watch him turn away; as you catch yourself watching the last flash of dark eyes, before they vanish beneath the hood he pulls over his head. You can't reach out to him, can't take any of this, and he will beckon you with dark glances and soft words, but you can't have anything. You own nothing, not property nor belongings. You carry your beliefs and you carry your devotion, but there is no room for anything else when your hands are so full of arrogance.

The last you saw of him was the night before you left, when you drank to fortune and brotherhood. You hadn't watched him as carefully as you should have, didn't see the things that lingered in front of you that he won't give voice to, and now you regret it. You regret not memorizing the curve of his smirk, the crinkle of it at the edges of his eyes; you regret not drinking it in now that you have ruined it beneath your own two hands. You leave his world and yours both equally in shambles.

You see him now and there is nothing left of the man who once welcomed you as a friend, nothing of the man you fought alongside, and there is nothing left of the man who had a place for you. The man who stands before you is drowning in anger, in regret and guilt, and he is suffocating on all of the pieces of his life that you left at his feet.

There is distance between you now that you could cover. You could cross the room and stop his retreat, to demand that he face you – that he face this anger, this strange tension. The hand he raises to the door you could take, could hold to your chest and show him the heartbeat you swear is still there. The repercussions you could withstand, could take without remorse, but you do not think you could swallow the way he would flinch away from you as though your touch is poison. There has not been enough time passed and he is not yours to hold. There is no room for you when his heart is filled with so much disgust.

The companionship that is between you now is brittle and tenuous – like a thread pulled tightly, eager to snap – and it is your own fault. He will help you when he has no other options, when it would hurt your mutual cause for him to scorn you, but his help will be reluctant and cold. To err is human and you nothing but. He will mend your wounds, berate you for your own spilled blood, and he will leave you laying on the floor like you are already dead to him; like there is nothing there worth saving. Regardless of his beliefs, regardless of the distance he tries to maintain, he will not let you die. He has always given in to you over and over, and even amidst his anger and his grief he cannot say 'no' to you.

There will come a time when you are capable of giving up everything. You will give up pride and honor, praise and jurisdiction, beliefs and fears. You will accept your disgraces and your dishonors, will allow them to make you humble, and you will rid your hands of the heavy arrogance and bitter pride that takes up so much of you. You will leave everything behind until you are completely empty, until there is nothing in you but a faint lingering reminder of what you once carried; faint and fainter until that too is gone. You will cling to the last remnant, cling to whatever remains, to what makes you yourself.

You will have nothing and it will make it easier when he reaches out to you, when he takes you in and accepts you for who you are, for who you've become. It will make it easier when he gives in to you, when he falls into you and your hands will be so empty that there will be nothing but room for him. You will reach that point, but you haven't yet. You watch him leave, because you are too young to realize your mistake – your mistakes – and because he is too stubborn to realize how to forgive you yet. You let him leave because you don't yet know how to make him stay.

Not Until the End
Mandi M. Lynch

You shake your hands, ball them into fists, and
repeat the motion over and over. You've been outside so
long that the gloves have stopped working, but you're too
numb to notice. They tried to take you with them, to get
you out of the cold, but you wouldn't go. At some point,
you noticed a long duster draped over your shoulders, and
you're grateful that it's big enough to fit over the coat
you're already wearing.

The first few snowflakes drop from the sky and you
shift your weight from left to right. One lands on your
nose.

In front of you, the workers are busy, and you
watch, spellbound to the scene in front of you. At the
start, you moved the first shovelful of dirt, then the second,
mumbling to yourself and depositing droplets of saltwater
on the fresh ground. After a while, you couldn't see the
cherry anymore, or the gleam of brass. When did they
take the shovel? You don't even remember walking over to
the drive, but you must have, because there you are, ten
feet away, watching.

There are four of them, still using shovels despite
the bulldozer behind them. You're sure it's for your

benefit, but you don't care. This chapter of your life is over, and you're waiting for them to finish the last page and close the book. They turn the shovels upside down and tap them on the pile, packing it in. Almost done now.

It only takes a dozen steps to get back to the site. The small, concrete slab has already been poured, and the boulder is waiting to be moved into place. It must weigh two hundred pounds or more, but you're determined. This is the last thing, and it should be you that does it, not some group of strangers getting paid fourteen dollars an hour and eager to get back home to their wives and kids and dogs. You finally get a grip on it, but you can't lift it.

One of them takes pitty and comes over to help you, silently grabbing most of the bulk from the other side, and you shuffle sideways; it's no quick task when the heels of your boots keep digging into the ground. But there it is, and you're finally over top of the concrete and can set it down. You meant to be gentle, to not drop it, but you still managed to chip off a small piece. Frustrated, you bend down and pick it up; only you would fuck up something this important. You kiss the fragment and slide it into your pocket, pushing away a dim thought about making it into a keychain or necklace later, such an interesting fragment of granite and all.

The flowers are behind you and again the workers step in to move them into place. You wave them off, and they give up and leave. You clearly want to do this without them, and you don't even register their footsteps or the moving of their equipment as you look at the array of colorful blooms. How do you do this? Haphazard? Is there some sort of system you weren't told about? Who should have told you? There were so many people, nameless, faceless, contracted in and out for the last three days. One of them surely should have said something. Right? Right?

You know you can't stand there all day, so you pick up the nearest box and start spreading the flowers out across the dirt. There's no method, no rhythm, but it feels right, so that's all that matters. One by one, you distribute them until the dirt is totally covered. Before you turn to leave, you see two roses in the bottom of a box, one red, one white.

Walking to the stone, you take the white one and kiss the cool rock as you lean over, gingerly placing the rose on top. The red one you pull up to your nose, and you take a minute to inhale the fragrant aroma of the bloom. Red – love, respect, courage. White – reverence, innocence, silence. The last two that you'll ever share.

And now, at last, you turn and walk away.

Family Line
Michele Berger

You barely notice your mother's tears and your father's solemn hug, on the Amtrak platform, as they release you into the muggy night. You're the oldest cousin and they say it's time for you to make this special trip. You overhear your mother say to your father, "Maybe, it's been long enough now and everyone's forgotten," but you don't pay it any attention. You're looking good in black jeans wearing a gold belt that spells Nate. You're eager to get to the next thing, even though your younger cousins Violetta, Corey, and Little Tate strike you as interesting as a drawer of socks. You've only met them once at a family reunion, their drawl and talk of porch sitting made little impression on you. You will call them 'bammas' as a matter of course. You're a sixteen year old Bronx boy about to visit your backwards cousins in North Carolina for the first time. A familiar twitchy feeling of restlessness runs through you like a racehorse that's been held at the gate too long.

*

You arrive and they love your wavy hair, your swagger, and your tales about spraying graffiti all over the city. By two weeks later, you've kissed all the hotties, rumbled with two guys and seen all the snakes, raccoons and trees that you can take. Just when you think you'll die of boredom sitting on their grand wraparound porch, Little Tate taps you on the shoulder and says, "We got a book— a special book." A year younger than you, but much taller and meatier—linebacker worthy, there's nothing little about him.

"This book is how Edward, one of our ancestors, got his freedom," Violetta chimes in with a dimpled smile. You peg her for slow because of her lisp and although twelve, she's babyish, wearing her hair in a one-sided ponytail.

"Never heard of-," you begin to say.

"Yeah, he stole *Beasts and Spells from the Savage Lands,* from his master's library and learned its secrets," Corey, Violetta's twin brother, interrupts, as he has been doing during your entire visit. A contrast to the steady mountain of Little Tate; Corey's jumpy, impatient, picking at scabs on his legs and arms when he's not running his mouth.

"Shut up, Corey," Violetta reprimands.

"Edward was an OG, original gangster," Little Tate says laughing.

You lean back in the chair and any lingering doubt about how stupid your cousins are vanishes. "Don't they teach you anything down here? Will you believe every dumb story you hear? Nobody ever earned their freedom with a book."

"Nate'd be afraid to see the book," Corey goads.

He jumps up and leans over you. He's in your face now and you want to slap him. He's a bully even without Little Tate's girth and confidence.

"Cousin probably ain't never even been in the woods at night. That and the book make you run for the next train to New York," Corey says.

"Me, scared of a book?" You howl with laughter and the pink Kool-Aid that you've been drinking snorts out your nose. "Are you crazy? Hell, I tag trains in the middle of the night. What's some old book to me? At home, I've got to deal with men who'll shoot me as soon as look at me."

Your cousins nod in unison and Little Tate looks satisfied as if he just scored a field goal.

*

And with the challenge in the air, the pack of cousins and you trudge through their woods to see the slave shack where this book lives. You've never been to a slave shack, or any shack. Although it's getting dark and pinpricks rise along the back of your neck, you say nothing. You're tough. And, besides they're just fucking with you, right?

The walk is short and soon you spy a building roughly framed and fashioned of unhewn logs chinked with mud, roofed with tarred clapboards.

"Edward's shack's was closest to the big house because he tended to the master often," Little Tate says.

"Big house burned down long time ago," Violetta adds as she opens the door.

Your eyes adjust as she lights two blue candles. Pitiful space, you note, not even the size of the smallest bathroom in your house. No furniture, just a mud floor, one window and musty rags moldering in crevices in the wall closest to you.

In the middle of the room an encyclopedia large, gilded, blue book sits open on a rotted log.

You're not surprised that a book is here, but nonetheless are impressed with its size. "So you put this book here? Just for me, huh? Probably got this from some used bookstore before I got here," you say.

"This is where the book stays," Corey says leaning down and brushing his fingertips across it.

"It's been in the family for *ever,*" Violetta says and she also bends down to touch the book. Her fingers glide across the width of it. Smoothing her skirt with care she makes a place for herself on the log.

"Never heard about it...besides slaves down here weren't taught to read," you say.

"Edward's master collected rare books and some slaves here could read and our Edward could read some," Corey answers you and gives a nod to his brother.

"Ever think about what you might do if you were a slave?" Little Tate asks.

For a moment, you finger your name belt and imagine everything about you stripped away and extinguished. A momentary panic shoots through like when you're running on the train tracks and it's dark and you have to make sure not to touch the third rail. One touch of the rail and you'd be gone. "I'd run, escape." That's what a racehorse would do, you think.

"Please," Little Tate says holding up a hand. "We all like to think we would've run. Some people did run, some people stayed-"

"Edward didn't do anything of those things!" Corey announces and is standing so close that some of his spit lands on your arm.

Violetta looks to the book and back to you as if she is waiting for something. You think what a good actress she is because she looks frightened.

"Edward called a beast up and it did his bidding," Little Tate says.

You lean in closer to the book trying to imagine your ancestor moving his mouth slowly over the words, on the pages, that looked like Old English—*betimes, shew, drync.* How did he do it, you wonder? How did he steal the book and when did he read it? Despite how ridiculous your cousins are being, a tiny bit of admiration for Edward is snaking up inside you.

"At first, it did," Violetta says, a nervous giggle and a belch escaping from her lips.

"What happened? you ask, "Edward start getting greedy?

"No, he asked for small stuff-- more cornmeal, a blanket, bowls," Little Tate says. Little Tate now bends down, just like his siblings did, and lingers on the pages of the book, turning some over.

"Then Edward tried his hand at bigger things, like asking for the overseer to get sick," Corey adds. You see how Corey's chest puffs out with pride as he talks.
At first you don't believe it...swirling blue mist is rising from the pages of the book. You squint looking around for the gizmos, wires, cables or machines that could produce this special effect. But you can't deny that you were sweating when you walked in and now the air feels cool in the shack. They are better at this hoodoo trick than you thought.

"It promised him things," Violetta says.

You flinch when Corey roars, "The beast said it would kill the master!"

"But, he wanted something in return," Violetta continues.

"A sacrifice," Little Tate says rising.

"Poor Edward had a son, Nate. He was sixteen, too," Violetta whispers. She gets up and stands next to Corey. She no longer seems little or someone to ignore. Corey and Violetta look united, purposeful. You wonder how long they have rehearsed this moment.

"I get it...This is where you're trying to scare the city kid!"

"No, that beast wanted the son. Edward gave him his son for us...so that we could be free. Edward started over again, a new man, with money and land. He did it for us," Corey says. Violetta reaches for his hand and he takes it and gives it a little shake.

"You're the special one. The beast waits for one boy in every generation," Little Tate says.

What you see forming in the mist makes you doubt everything you know. A faint shape. Familiar...from field trips to museums. Dogs of Egypt. Anubis? Book of the Dead. The weighing of the heart. Hermanubis. Half-man, half-jackal. It's the head of a large jackal, its muzzle a yellow and dull gray. Soon its white torso appears. Its presence fills the room. You notice its pointed salmon colored tongue, drooling saliva.

Violetta is the first to weep and shuts her eyes. She leans into Corey for a moment, 'They never told us it was so big."

"Shut up!" Corey says through clenched teeth and wide-eyed.

You rush head long for the door and smack into the bulk of Little Tate.

With studied ease he turns you, holding you firmly under the neck and arm.

"You're going do this right, Nate. We have to do this, just like our parents did."

"And those before them," Corey says.

And, now you remember your mother's last embrace, holding on so tight like she'd lose you forever. And, the quiet stories at family gatherings of distant uncles and cousins, all dying young --by drowning, car accidents, and disappearances and always in North Carolina.

"But...but, we've been free...are free, " your dry mouth mumbles.

"Beast don't care," Corey says now with a self-assured laugh.

"Hey, hey...you can make a different choice," you say straining against your cousin's grip hearing the pleading in every word you utter.

"Who knows what'll happen if we don't offer someone up. What we'll lose?" Corey says.

Little Tate's lips brush against your ear, "He's family; just like you," he whispers.

In the struggle, you start to wonder--What had you done with all that freedom you had gathering up around you like pools of unused stretchable fabric?

Little Tate releases you back to the center of the room. As Corey's knife rams into your collarbone and you fall, you see no doubt in your cousin's eyes. You see a beast's shadow and madness.

You thought you might die along train tracks running from the police, or shot for your sneakers. Lots of people die for stupid reasons. For less than this, you think. For less wisdom, for less freedom, for less than Edward's tenacity. Your blood finds its way down your chest, to your stomach and drips into the belt buckle. You clutch it. I am Nate. I am free now and will die free. Not a simple racehorse anymore, you think. As you slip away, you ponder what it will be like to be a blood racehorse running through the veins of your family line, circulating through time to keep their freedom alive.

Strawberry Girl

Pamela Scott

She's the new girl in school. For months she doesn't know you exist. You're just another blurred face in the crowds. She races past you in the halls without as much as a second glance.

You see her all right. Your big eyes take in everything. Her tiny little waist, the curves of her hips, her slender legs, her sweet little mouth, the way her hair bounces when she walked and how she always smells like Peppermint.

You follow her everywhere. You hang outside her classes clutching your notebook against your chest, peek at her between rows of boring old textbooks in the school library and watch her eat her lunch in the canteen.

You scribble her name in your English jotter in crazy looping swirls. Karen. Karen Anne Turner. Karen Turner. K Turner. Karen and Lucy. Lucy and Karen. K & L 4-Ever. L & K 4-Ever.

You almost die the first time she speaks to you. You're drawing a picture of her in your art notebook. You watch as she flirts with boys in the year above and smokes. She asks if you want a draw and you tale one. You've never smoked before and choke and splutter. She laughs and ruffles your hair.

Over time you become friends. She starts smiling at you in the corridor, says hello every other day, asks to borrow your pen, wants to know what time it is, shares your notes on Shakespeare and sits beside you during lunch.

You whisper to each other at the back of the class, make up stories about the other students, create joke names for the teachers, bitch about prettier girls, swap anecdotes on cute boys you have crushes on but your eyes never really leave her face.

One hot day you eat strawberries in a field across from your house. You lie on your backs and stare up at the hot sun. There's a basket full of juicy red fruit sat on the ground between you. You feed the soft, tender berries to each other. Your mouths, fingers and T-shirt's are stained red. You watch every bite she takes; the rise and fall of her hands, the movement of her jaw and the crunching of her teeth. Sweet red juice runs down her chin and you ache to lick it away. You eat too many strawberries. Your stomach aches so much it hurts to move. You stare up at the bright yellow sun and wonder if it really can burn your eyes.

She tells you about Mark in the year above. All the girls fancy him. He has greasy black hair and a big spot on the end of his nose. She tells you about the day he put his thing inside her at the underpass while his friends watched. You hate him and wish him dead. You hope his spot takes over his face, his skin rots and falls off and his thing turns black and drops off.

The next day you let him put his thing inside you. You want to feel everything she's touched. He grunts in your ear and calls you sweetheart. You imagine her hands in place of his. You tell her about it after school lying on her pink bed. You compare notes. You make jokes about how small his thing is.

You can't stop looking at her. Her skin's lovely and soft. She never has a spot. Her teeth are beautiful and white. She smells so good it makes you dizzy. She always has a few strands of hair hanging over her face. You want to brush them away but you're never brave enough.

During sleepovers you lie as close to her as you dare. You smell her. Her scent makes you dizzy. She smells like Peppermints and creamy soap. You press your face against her hair. When she takes your hand in the dark you feel giddy. You lie trembling next to her quietly dying.

You can't sleep at night for thinking about her. You lie awake shaking, trembling and sweating. You think about her lips, her smell, the way she looks in tight jeans, the curve of her spine and how she walks. You want to kiss her. You want to roll around on the grass with her. You want to touch her like Mark did. You want to smell her hair. You want to hold her in your arms. You press your hot face into the cold sheets until you fall asleep.

She says you're blood sisters. You cut your palms with slivers of broken glass. You press the wounds together and mix your blood. She says you'll be together forever and nothing but death can keep you from each other.

You start dressing alike. You wear your hair the same way. You go everywhere together. People call you the Terrible Twosome. She sleeps over every other night. The other kids think you're both weird but you don't care. You have each other. You carve her name into the trunk of an old tree.

She starts going steady with Mark. They hold hands in the corridor, kiss all the time and she laughs at his stupid jokes. He's always pawing her. She drapes herself all over him. You want him to drop dead of a wasting disease. You make little wax models of him and melt them in the microwave.

She comes to you the day he dumps her. She tells you what a pig he is. She saw him snogging Nora in the year above. Nora has big breasts and dyed hair. She sobs in your arms, begs you never to leave her and asks you not hurt her like him.

She kisses you first. The kiss is just like you imagined. It's soft and perfect like air brushing your mouth, wet and kind of hot. Her mouth's sticky. The kiss takes your breath away. You feel your body rise twelve feet in the air. You feel all shaky. She smells like strawberries. Your hands slip naturally around her waist.

She doesn't stop you. She wraps her body around you. You run your fingers through her hair. She asks you to kiss her all over, touch her, make her giggle, make his sweaty smell go away, tell her she's pretty, tell her she's better looking than Nora, Nora's a dog and she's the queen bee. You tell her what she wants to hear.

You both lie down on top of your bed. You kiss for a long time. You think how different it feels from kissing boys. Right somehow. Her lips are soft, warm and lovely. Boys are sweaty and wet. They try to stick their tongue down your throat. Boys are horrible. You slip your hands under her T-shirt. Her body's hot. She's sweating. Her skin's clammy. She moans and you move your hands further. She freezes.

She asks what you're doing and looks scared. Words choke in your throat. Her big, wide eyes stare up at you. You see panic in them. You don't understand what's happened. She asks you again. Her voice's loud, hysterical. You shake your head, bewildered.

She shoves you backwards. The force makes you slam your head against the wall. You scream in pain. She cries out in terror. She calls you a 'bitch' and a 'cow' and a 'dirty slut'.

She wants to know why you put your hands on her. You can't think of a thing to say. She hits you in the face, slaps you hard enough to leave a mark then runs from the room sobbing. You hear her footsteps on the stairs. The front door opens and slams.

When she's gone you slam every door in the house, run back up to your bedroom, lock the door and turn the CD player on, listen to some slush by Boyzone and threw yourself on top of your bed. You punch your pillow over and over with both fists. You scream your rage into the empty room. You moan her name, sob, shriek like a mad woman and roar until your throat dries up and a bubble of snot forms in the corner of one nostril.

You tear up the unsent love letters you wrote to her, the pages of soppy poetry, the doodles, the pictures of you laughing together and your journal. You bundle it all into the coal fire downstairs and watch it burn. You keep one picture of you both and hide it away so you'll always have a part of her.

You see a big truck parked in front of her house a few days later. STELLA'S REMOVALS is painted on the side. You watch her family pile boxes inside. She turns towards the window and your eyes lock. She's carrying a big pile of books. You stare each other out. Her eyes are red and swollen. You know she's been crying. She walks away. You watch as the van drive off and something dies inside you.

This is how you remember her: tall, too thin, long shapely legs, tiny little waist, standing in the street with her arms full of books, looking up at your window with the sun shining on her hair and making her head look like it was on fire.

Your strawberry girl.

The Guy That the Other Guy Fell On, or Vice Versa

Robert J. Krog

You were on a horse, you see. You were on a horse, or you were nearby when they rode near on the horses. Well, it was one or the other. And you hit your head when you fell off the horse, or at any rate when someone on a horse fell off on top of you. But, at any rate, you hit your head. And that's why you have insomnia. Or is it called something ending in -ack? You hit your head and got hypochondriac. That might be it. Maybe it's called insomnia. That's it. Yes. Insomnia.

And now, you're a hero. Well, the guy who fell off the horse is a hero. That's you though, right? Well, it's either you or the guy you fell on. But, why worry about that? You're a hero after all.

You aren't making any sense, are you?

Your name? Names are very important. The guy on the horse certainly has a name. Everybody does, of course. And the guy on the ground who got landed on by the guy on the horse, well, he has a name too. What was it? Something plain like Bob or Joe. It could have been Bubba. The guy on the horse? He has a name, for sure. What could it be? It's something grand. Cervantes, perhaps. Maybe Goethe. Could be Napoleon, or Genghis. Well, it's a very fine name. The point is, everybody has a name, even you. You just don't know what it is, because you have insomnia. You'll remember it eventually. Probably. Sometimes that happens. Sometimes. Not to worry.

But how did it all happen? You already know. You either fell off a horse on to some guy and bumped your head, or some guy on a horse fell off it onto you and you bumped your head, and then you got hypochondriac and forgot your name and how you got here. Silly, yes?

That doesn't help much, does it?

Wait, you can recall. You can do it. It went like this. There was a fellow on a horse - you already know about him - and he was riding along trying to save a girl, which he did do and that's what makes him a hero - or you are a hero - it might be you, mightn't it? At any rate, he was riding along on his horse, chasing the bad fellow - do you know about the bad fellow? The one who kidnapped the girl in the first place? He was on a horse in front of the other fellow - might have been you - and had the girl, the one he'd kidnapped, across his saddle in front of him, and he was being chased by the first fellow, the hero - might be you - and trying like heck to get away with the girl he'd kidnapped, the one across his saddlebow.

Your story could be a little more concise and clear, it's true.

Very well, you were riding along like heck, too, trying to catch the guy who had kidnapped the girl. Of course, you might have just been standing there and a guy fell on you. You might have been that guy, but it's so hard to tell. It'd be much easier if you didn't have insomniarhea and no memory of what you were doing there.

Some tea? Yes, you'd like some tea. You're probably a big tea drinker. Tea is good for memory, or so you've been told.

Well, back to your story. You were supposed to have married the girl, but the other guy - the fellow on the horse in front, you know - he had always thought he'd the right to marry her, which everybody says he didn't, because she told him 'No. N, O. No.' And it was your wedding day, yours and the girl's, you together, or the guy on the horse chasing the other guy anyway. It was his wedding and the girl's or yours and the girls, one or the other.

But back to your story. The guy who wanted her but didn't get her; he showed up uninvited and unannounced and crashed the wedding. That's what the say, 'crashed the wedding,' as if it were a vase or something that could be thrown on the floor and crashed into a thousand pieces. Doesn't make much sense that expression, but that's what they say, 'crashed the wedding.' He showed, up, the fellow who did the kidnapping, and he kidnapped the girl. Well, it wasn't that easy, was it? You, or that other guy, whichever it was, you didn't put up with that, and neither did your groomsmen, or his groomsmen if that's whose they were, and the guy who did the kidnapping - Do you know? He's got a name, too. It's something sinister, probably Frank or Bill. Could be Maude. That's a woman's name, of course, but it has a sinister ring to it. But it was probably, Coriolanus, come to think of it. Everybody's got a name, even you. You just don't remember what it is, because you hit your noggin, and have insomniacrid. Well, Frankestro, he had a sword. Lot's a men carry swords. It's all the fashion these days to be carrying swords and challenging other men to duels, usually young men, but there were those two octegenericans who had a duel the other day and fell down a hill together into a pond. They lost their swords and both of them broke legs. No, actually, one broke both his legs and the other sprained his wrist. But, at any rate, lots of men carry swords and Coriolanky and you both had yours, and so did your groomsmen. Well, if it was you. Don't forget now, you could just be that guy that the other guy fell on and made you hit your head.

Where has your story gone now? Right. Coriolanus showed up, and he had his sword. The groomsmen, well they all jumped up and drew their swords - actually, one of them had an axe, and another one just had a dagger. The rest of them - he had a sword, too. It was a very big sword. A claymore or a - one of those things it takes two hands to wield. Could have been a rapier. They all look alike, really - sharp, pointy, edges and all that, the thing you grip with your hand. He had a sword.

He wasn't very good with it. Billister cut him down fast. Or was his name Coriolanus? Everybody has a name. The guy with the sword - the groomsmen, not Coriolankus - he had a name. It was something friendly, like Bull or Fred.

Your story? Your story, indeed. Where has your story gone? So, the guy who did the kidnapping, he chopped the groomsmen up proper. You were a little ways off when it all started, when Bulliolanus came in and did the chopping on your groomsmen. Of course, you're presuming that you are the hero, which is really a bit presumptuous. You could just be the guy that the other guy fell on and made you hit your head. But, well, maybe you are the bridegroom hero, fella.

Sugar? You like sugar in your tea? So you do. Yes, sugar please. Lot's of folks like sugar in their tea. Tea's good for the memory. You need tea.

Where has your story gone? So. She didn't put up much of a fight. Could have been that wedding dress. It was cumbersome. She's a spirited girl and not prone to be manhandled, but to give him credit, Bullfrankers threw her right onto his horse and was off before you could get over there to stop him.

You, or that other guy, jumped on your horse and followed. You had your groomsman's axe in one hand and your own big, meat cleaver in the other and the reins in your teeth - that might be why you fell off your horse. They say a good rider can steer a horse with his knees, though. That's what they say, but you did fall off your horse, or that other guy did, one or the other.

No matter, though. That's not where your story is. You must have patience with memory. Drink more tea. It's almost to that point.

You chased them down fast and threw your axe at Frankestro. You missed, in point of fact. The axe struck a tree and stayed there, pretty as a picture and all, but it definitely missed what you were aiming to hit. Don't feel bad, however. It might not have been you that missed. You might just be that guy that the other guy fell on.

Where has your story gone? You were chasing the guy that did the kidnapping down, you know, Frankello? Him. Right. And you'd thrown your axe at him and missed. Embarrassing, of course, but you were much too angry to feel embarrassed, or maybe missing made you even angrier. You weren't thinking too clearly, it's clear, because you fell on that other guy, or he fell on you. Whichever it was, there was a guy who fell - could've been you - and there was a guy that got fallen on - also could have been you.

So, there you were, just missed the kidnapper, Frankaghengis, because the axe hit a tree instead of him. You still had your sword. You waved it about as you drew up alongside the kidnapper, the guy who thought he ought to get to marry the girl but didn't. You remember him, Corioghenhis? You were going to swipe his head off, and he was so busy struggling with the girl that he couldn't get his sword out. You had a clear shot at his head and neck and all, but your sword hit a tree, too. Wouldn't you know it? That's when you fell of your horse.

Or the other guy fell on you. Are you making this up, or remembering? You can't make this kind of stuff up, can you?

More tea? Yes, you'd like more tea. Tea is good for the memory, or so you've been told.

What were doing in there way anyhow? Most people, when they see other people on horses galloping right at them like mad, which they were, being a kidnapper and an offended bridegroom whose bride had been kidnapped, get out of the way.

So, getting bearings on your story again, this is how it went. You fell off the horse when your sword got stuck in the tree. You probably held onto it too hard. That seems the likeliest explanation. And there was this guy on the ground, trying to duck behind the same tree the sword got stuck in - seems likely doesn't it - and you fell on him. Could've been you that were trying to duck behind the tree, though. Yet, you might be the hero or just the innocent bystander trying not to get trampled. It's hard to say.

Where has your story gone? There's the girl, naturally. She's still in danger. Well, this is what happened. The kidnapper, his throat really was all exposed to a blow. When your blow with your sword didn't fall on his neck, she punched him in the neck with her fist. Her hand became free when he let go of it to try to get his sword so he could fight you, not that he needed to worry about that, mind you.

She punched him hard. He might be dead. Nobody checked too much on him. He just lay there like a pole axed fish. You, they were concerned about, and the guy that fell off the horse. You were addled. You're still addled. The girl was fine, some bruising from being belly first on a galloping horse, but fine, really. She had to go get her dress sewn up. It has some tears in it, as you can well imagine. The bridesmaids whisked her away, her protestations notwithstanding. Brides do a lot of protesting. Some of them are downright mean. She seemed more concerned.

There was a bride in the next county who protested the color of her dress, the color of the flowers - nothing matched her bridegrooms eyes, despite all her planning - you know how brides do all that planning - or maybe not, just having a bridegroom fall on you doesn't let you know all about a weddings - but she finally just made him change his eye color. You might remember the story if you ever recover from your insomnophelia.

Why anyone would pole axe a fish, though, that it is a question. Netting a fish seems more proper. Pole axing doesn't make any sense. If you were fishing, you'd use a net, for sure.

How to Move Your Parents Out of the Family Home

Sharon Goldberg

Volunteer to fly 3,000 miles cross country and spend two weeks sorting through everything your parents have accumulated during the past fifty-two years. Plan to stage a garage sale. When you arrive, take one look at the two-car garage with barely room for a bicycle and reconsider.

Tackle the kitchen first. Take inventory of all pots and pans, dish sets, cutlery, serving bowls, platters, TV trays, small appliances (Did they ever use the Santa Fe Quesadilla Maker you bought?), Tupperware, towels, pot holders, tablecloths, placemats, and matching napkins. Set aside the bare minimum—the Willow Creek Senior Residence serves breakfast and dinner daily—and place the balance in boxes for the five grandchildren who now live in their own apartments. Tell your mom, thank you very much, you sincerely appreciate the offer, but you don't want your grandmother's sterling silver flatware or anything else silver because it requires polishing. Quickly assure her that you will cherish Grandma's "Mona Lisa" needlepoint and hang it above your fireplace.

Suggest that your parents discard all issues of Architectural Digest, National Geographic, Sports Illustrated, and Modern Maturity published before the year 2000. Convince them to dump any magazine published before the Viet Nam War.

Recommend that your father sell his stamp collection. When he balks, encourage him to at least toss the tiny waxed paper envelopes, catalogs, and other collection paraphernalia stuffed in his desk drawers.

Throw away all duplicates and triplicates of family photos from the 1950s that your mom never sent to relatives as promised. Don't tell your parents. Also get rid of any photos of people neither your mom nor dad can identify. (Who's that man leering at your mom, his arm around her shoulder, nearly touching her breast? "Just a friend," she says.)

Insist that your dad discard all expired coupons in his alphabetized file, along with any for pet food, frozen pizza, or Tampax, none of which he or your mom now use. Remind him it's no longer practical to buy fruit juice, tuna fish, and paper towels in bulk. Apologize for being pushy and insensitive.

Offer the sterling silver to your sister-in-law. Apologize for not asking your mother first. Retract the offer.

Ask your two brothers to clear their stuff out of your parents' closets and basement—this includes ancient baseball gloves and Wiffle balls, yearbooks, award-winning elementary school art and science projects, ashtray and shot glass collections, and the guitar your older brother tried to craft during his hippie days. Remove your own prom dresses, majorette baton, sorority paddle, and ugly or useless wedding gifts you never returned and promised to ship to your own home long ago. Laugh and reminisce as you show your parents your scrapbooks filled with party invitations, dried corsages, cocktail napkins, band concert programs, pictures from the senior class play, "Arsenic and Old Lace," in which you starred, and strawberry rolling papers from the first time you smoked pot (whoops!).

Tell your mom, thank you very much, you sincerely appreciate the offer, but you don't want the twelve matching crystal wine glasses she purchased in Austria and doesn't use anymore ("Who is there to invite? Our friends are dead or in Florida.") Ask if you can offer them to your sister-in-law.

Pare down the memorabilia hanging on the walls— an embroidered sampler: "If Mother Says No, Ask Grandmother," your mom's Associate Degree from Lorain County Community College (Cum Laude), your dad's PWT (Putting Wife Through) degree from the same school, your mom's Red Cross Volunteer commendation, your dad's Rotary Life Membership certificate and his Ohio Bar Association Fifty-Year award. Listen to your dad's story about the night he received the legal honor and Congressman Eric Brown shook his hand. Start to cry when you see your mom crying.

Box up most of the hardback books from shelves in the family room and donate them to the public library, historical society, and Boys and Girls Club. Throw out millions of shopping bags, grocery bags, dry cleaning bags, yellowed greeting cards, and gift tags. Give most of the plants to the neighbors.

Ask your brothers when they're going to move their junk.

Help your parents pare down their clothing, Mom's hat collection, and Dad's decades of neckties. Keep a few of your mother's sweaters that you've always admired and a funky paisley blouse from the 1960s that's back in style. Reminisce when you discover the dress your mom wore to your wedding twenty-eight years ago, the blue uniform she wore when she was a Cub Scout den mother, the powder blue leisure suit your father wore the summer they vacationed in Hawaii. Ask your dad if he ever slept in the navy blue silk pajamas you found in the back of the closet. "Oh, once or twice," he says. He winks at your mom. Get upset when your mom tries to give you her good jewelry. Tell her you don't want it now, she's moving, not dying; she'll still dress up and go out. "It's not so easy anymore," she says. "I spend half the day in the bathroom."

Drink a glass of wine and assess the garage. Designate for disposal four green vinyl kitchen chairs (ripped), a thirty-six-cup Farberware coffee urn (broken), a Mr. BBQ rolling grill (obsolete), a roll of golden beige carpet (remnants), two brown leather suitcases (scratched), decorations from your mom's sixty-fifth birthday party (silly), a redwood picnic bench (splintered), six window screens (rusty), three file cabinets (dented), and a foot-operated Singer sewing machine that belonged to your Great Aunt Sarah. Ask your younger brother to give away Dad's golf clubs since he's no longer in condition to use them.

Emphasize that your parents' new apartment is one-third the size of their home so they can only fit one-third of the furniture inside. Arrange for Goodwill to pick up the queen-sized sofa bed, maple wood credenza, four swivel bar stools, walnut dressers and night stands from the room your brothers shared, and the French provincial canopy bed you slept in as a teenager.

Tell your mother you've decided you want Grandma's silver after all. She hugs you.

Inform your brothers it's been five days and to get their shit out of the house now or you'll burn it.

At the end of your second week back home, supervise the movers as they load your parents' remaining possessions in a van. "Don't break anything," your mom says to the men. Join your parents on a final walk through the now naked home where they spent most of their married years, where you and your brothers grew up, where the family gathered for birthdays and anniversaries and holidays. Your mom clutches her walker. Your dad leans on his cane. Hunched in the middle of the living room, he says, "That's it."

The three of you walk out the front door together.

3:07 PM

Simone Martel

You run out of the concrete-block building, onto the hot playground, your limp hair stuck behind your ears, a sweater lashed round your middle.

"Wait, you guys!" you call to the other girls, racing toward the street. You have stop to rearrange the lunch box, workbooks, construction paper pumpkins and plush rabbit in your arms.

Shrill cries fly back at you: "We'll miss the bus!"

Threats: "You better come on!"

"Fine!" you say, running after them. Then you drop your rabbit. When you pick it up again, you find Velvet Ear's pink velour fur powered with playground dirt. You brush her with a sticky finger, rubbing it in. Smudged and matted, her fur will never stand up and sparkle again. You want to howl: no fair! But there's no one to yell it to, no arms to scoop up your junk and bustle you along with three fingers pressed into your back. You can't close your eyes and open your mouth and wail yourself away from the hot playground. You understand: that's your real burden. You're on your own, with years of messing up ahead of you. That knowledge makes you plant your feet

apart and set your sweaty, round face against the sun. You
hug your bundles and run hard to catch the school bus
home.

Five Easy Steps
Søren G. Palmer

You take a shot before he comes over. You cover
the bottom of a short glass with a pool of Grey Goose
vodka then dump it down your throat. It burns, of course,
and you consider another but need to be numb, not drunk.
He's coming to break up with you, and if you want him
back this is the first and most important of five easy steps.
Without perfect execution of step one, what was simply a
small puddle between you and step two becomes Lake
Superior. And you're not such a good swimmer.

You step into the silk red pajama bottoms that
make your ass look fabulous. While touching up your eyes
and adding some gloss to your lips you consider the
possibility that you are wrong. That the meat grinder in
your stomach is related to something else, that the reason
he hasn't wanted to have sex with you in eleven days – a
record, to be sure – is because he really is tired, that he
hasn't reached across the table and gently pushed your
bangs behind your ears in eighteen days because they've
actually been behaving. But your bangs never behave and
the meat grinder has proven efficient from Scott Hellman
in the sixth grade to that diver in college, the one who
could do amazing things with his body. You twirl your hair

into a bun on top of your head and grab a brown clip from the towel rack, its teeth scraping your skull as it bites down.

You turn on both lamps, are putting your briefcase and a few books in the big chair so he has to sit by you on the couch when there is a knock on the door. You pull your bare feet off the floor, slipping them underneath you and grab The Sweet Hereafter off the coffee table. You remind yourself: do not ask him why he knocked, do not ask him why he is doing this, and above all else, do not cry. Five easy steps become ten difficult ones if you cry.

He is dressed casually in jeans and a black, long sleeve Tee. It is a kind of armor, protecting him from your emotions. If you didn't want him back you'd cry, cry a fucking river his self image would spend the next month treading water in. He says hello and walks straight into the kitchen then back into the living room. This is good humor, so you wait a few minutes while he paces, before patting the couch next to you.

He finally sits, and rubs the skin on his forehead. His eyebrows need to be trimmed, two hairs in particular are longer than the rest. He's mumbling now, trying to sand down the points of his words, which would be kind if it wasn't for his own benefit: guys don't make women cry. You tell him to hold that thought – even it's a live fish in his hands – and walk in front of him to the bathroom so he gets a good look at your ass and return with scissors. You trim one of the hairs, just to make him wait, but leave the other. Then you sit on your feet again and tell him to go on, opening and closing the scissors.

When he finally says it – I need to not be with anyone right now – it does sting and you do want to cry so you pretend you are arranging your feet and pinch the skin between your fingernails, hard. Thank God, you say, you've been thinking the same thing for a few weeks now, maybe a month, but haven't had the courage to bring it up. You remove the clip and shake your hair down past your shoulders. I always knew you were braver than me, you tell him, reaching over and patting his knee.

He looks like a bird that has flown into a sliding glass door. It's almost cute, and you consider snipping that last insolent hair when the meat grinder sticks on an emotion, reminding you that you still have been dumped and still would like to cry, are in fact going to cry as soon as he walks out of the door so you ask him if there's anything else. Anything else? he repeats. Yes, you say standing up to show him the door, that you want to talk about. He doesn't move.

This should be his biggest wet dream: you aren't crying and he can leave. But he's starting to explain. My life is moving in a different direction . . . This is insulting. And patronizing. And it makes you want to stab him with the scissors, but that isn't part of step one. Your routine has been flawless up to this point, a perfect ten, and it would be a shame to ruin all that with some blood and a trip to the ER. He's still talking, looking at the floor, that one hair appears to be growing, hardening, a horn shooting straight from his head.

You walk towards the door. There is a little blood on top of your foot – you pinched too hard – and you wonder if your open-toed Stuart Wietzman's will cover it, you were going to wear them tomorrow. You put your hand on the doorknob. The next four steps are so simple: don't contact him for two weeks; send an e-mail admitting mistakes you've been able to see (even though there aren't any); sleep with one of his friends (but not a good friend); sleep with him but do not go down on him, and make sure you tell him, this doesn't mean we're back together (even though it does) and that it was better than before (even though it won't be). But here he is, ruining all that by swimming around in his own pity. You see step two, an empty bottle in the middle of a lake, filling up with water.

Delayed

Susan Koefod

Your finger is positioned on the shutter of your cell phone camera. You stand on one foot, and with your other foot you depress the toilet's "flush" button while simultaneously pressing the camera shutter. You stand as still as you can and film the action of the automated toilet seat cover snaking around the seat. You let go of the shutter when the fresh seat cover is in place.

It took you several tries before you perfectly filmed the action of the mechanical seat cover. The lighting wasn't the best in the original stall you selected, so you moved to one right under the skylight, adjusted your shooting position several times so your shadow wouldn't get in the way, and finally you had it. A You-tube-worthy film of O'Hare's famous automated toilet seat covers.

You insert the movie file into a text, and send your cell phone toilet cover movie to your family. It's been hours since they asked for an update on when you would finally be home. You suspect this will tell them what they need to know.

You'd been stranded at O'Hare for hours, having missed your connection because of two mechanical problems on your inbound flight. While you had received frequent updates from the gate agent, who explained that mechanics were waiting for a part, and thought it would only be a few minutes before the part arrived, it actually turned out to be a couple of hours for the part to be installed, but none of that matters now. You also heard numerous apologies for the inconvenience. However, nothing was actually ever done to alleviate that inconvenience.

And now, you have only yourself to blame for the inconvenient way your day has turned out.

For you are not the obnoxious woman who sat a few rows behind you on your delayed inbound flight while it was still at the gate: this was the woman who very loudly INSISTED on her cell phone to a "very pleasant" customer service representative -- and then to that pleasant customer service representative's supervisor -- that she immediately be rebooked with a confirmed seat on the VERY NEXT FLIGHT in the connecting city. She threatened some follow-up action that had very serious consequences, though she didn't specify what either the actions or those consequences were.

You ended up hoping they would get her the damn seat so she would shut up.

Still you were not so bold as to turn around in your seat and see if the obnoxious woman looked how you had imagined her: like an overfed bulldog wearing one of those gaudy, rhinestone collars, maybe with a matching scarf.

You finally got a chance to see her, precisely two hours and fourteen minutes later (or four hours after your flight was originally scheduled to land in your connecting city). You spotted her immediately: she was the one triumphantly marching off the jet way with the bulldog swagger only those with confirmed seats possess.

Another reason this debacle is your fault because you are also not the very sexy, leggy, elite frequent flyer who immediately rebooked to another airline the moment the word "DELAYED" lit at the departure gate. She was the one with the ear buds casually draped around her neck, the chic outfit, the cute boots, and the perfectly tied scarf. This was the woman who simultaneously carried on a flirtatious banter with another elite frequent flyer guy, sent a gazillion texts from her Blackberry, and probably closed some international business deal worth millions. Leggy frequent flyer headed off with elite guy to a different gate, and you wondered whether they would connect later.

No. You are neither a demanding loudmouth nor a sophisticated and hot elite flyer. You are a casual traveler. You are doomed to spend a full day in Chicago's United Terminal, as the only flight you are confirmed on is the last flight out of the day. This sad truth will cause you, more than once, to realize you would have gotten home far sooner by renting a car and driving the 10 hours from your departure city to your destination: home.

And so you resign yourself, reconfiguring your day with the knowledge that everything is out of your hands. You're stuck. You run into the people bumped from your flight: the hapless, style-less, clueless travelers who insisted on nothing for themselves and therefore got nothing. You notice that some could use deodorant, and you sniff the air around yourself to make sure you are not the offending party.

You try the world's best caramel corn, and buy three huge tins to bring home for the kids, which you wind up lugging awkwardly all day long through one of the world's largest air terminals. You dine on hotdogs they claim are the same as those sold at Wrigley Field. You find yourself thinking about the Chicago Cubs. You realize that it isn't coincidental that the purgatory known as O'Hare is in the city of a baseball team whose fans are known for their steadfastness, despite years of defeat.

You think about drinking a lot and perhaps even more. Why not? You've got an entire day to kill. But the bars are crowded, and there are long lines of people waiting to get in. For a time, you sit on the outside edge of the mechanical walkway as there are no empty chairs to be found, anywhere. You watch people sliding by you and wonder how many of them missed their connecting flights and are entertaining themselves by riding back and forth on the moving walkway.

Eventually you find yourself in a toilet stall, snapping cell phone movies of the automated toilet seat covers. You look up through the bathroom skylight to the empty sky high above the airport bathroom. You see a solitary plane entering one corner of the skylight, thousands of feet above it, so far away that it looks no larger than a gnat. You point your cell phone camera at it, hit the shutter, and capture its unapologetic flight across the blameless blue sky.

Maintenance
-or-
How to Spend a Perfect Night in New Orleans
Theresa Tumminello Brader

Meet your best friend in front of his unrented, self-renovated double shotgun as the early September sun starts to set. Watch his face as he asks for a hug and then asks again. Admire, but don't focus on, the new multicolored fleur-de-lis attic window he points out to you. (Thoughts of attics panic you.) Before you follow him down the side of the house, stop him in the narrow passageway shaded by the neighboring two-story. Hug him, right there, behind the closed gate he repaired the hinges of while waiting for you to arrive.

You notice the empty doghouse in the backyard before you register the wrought-iron table holding a plastic cup, a plate of cheese crackers and a lighted candle inside a rosy votive holder. Exclaim over his sweetness—be certain you speak to his good ear—and give him another hug. He replies no, you're the sweet one, for coming to visit him. His embraces cause the fake magnolia (the first

Katrina-related fundraising item you've bought, but not the last) to slip from your hair. Clip it to his work shirt.

Tour one side of the shotgun, your guide first showing you how high the waterline was after the storm. Kiss him in the room where y'all made love several years ago. His fingers descend and you pull away to apologize for no longer owning any sexy underwear, knowing he's going to tell you to shush up and kiss him. His fingers move and you sharply draw in your breath. You're amused by his satisfied chuckle.

He leads you back outside to sit at the table. The surrounding houses create a snug enclave fit for two, the dusky sky its endless vaulted ceiling. You're too excited to be hungry (like a flighty mouse, you only nibble at the crackers), but agree to split a burger with him at a lounge on Canal Street. Take the go-cup of vodka and cranberry juice with you.

As y'all walk, you each share an explicit memory of lovemaking from years ago. He relates the anticipation he felt every time he knocked on the door of your own shotgun (now lost to you), how his heart jumped as the door opened on your smile. (Across the street the tombs peeking above the mausoleum barely catch your eye, but later you'll be able to recall the precise timbre of his voice.) You feel nostalgic and tell him so as he holds open for you the glass door of the nightclub. (Later, you'll understand that indulging in nostalgia wards off painful reflections of the more recent past.)

Sit at the crowded bar, order a draft of Abita Amber (gulping an icy mouthful settles you down) and talk with your best friend about everything. Stroke his knee. He tells you he likes that. Do it again. Lean in and interrupt him to say you want to kiss him. His face, startled and grinning, expresses his pleasure this time. Y'all leave quickly after eating and then retrace your steps while touching hands in the shadows of the streetlights.

Follow him into the other half of the shotgun (the side with a bed), where y'all undress and shower in the clawfoot bathtub. Rub soap on each other. Under the showerhead, kiss him until, pulling away to turn off the old-fashioned taps, he says that's it, he's done.

Get in bed; this time he follows you. Obey the words in your ear: they tell you to open your eyes and see how beautiful y'all are together. In the mirror two heads belong to one body moving in rhythm, faces soft in the digital-lit darkness, a mass of unruly curls under a resilient chin, his arms flanking yours.

You're emotional, as if you might both laugh and cry (the way you feel when you recognize a story you've labored over is finally finished), and you tell him you love him. He says your voice seems different and you realize it's because you want to scream—a scream of release.

A frisson runs through you and you can't stop trembling. His arms wrap around you, constrain you from disintegrating. Listen to his voice (it's your favorite sound of all) and, as he speaks, the shattered fragments of your self cohere.

Sudden rain patters the roof and you wish he heard it too. He massages your scalp and neck, and, when you say you have to leave soon, he exclaims that he thought you were spending the night. Laugh and sigh, yearning for it to be true. After your best friend threatens to make love to you again if you stay much longer, you lie back down.

Lives Parallax

M.V. Montgomery

In another universe, you had an extra brother,
and your godfather wasn't killed in a plane crash,
and your brother and his wife didn't bury their first child.

In a second universe, you did, after all,
get your first girlfriend pregnant, then married her,
and lived in a rock-and-roll house full of kids.
You also managed a restaurant.

Against all odds, yours was the marriage
others looked up to and thought, rock solid,
and your wife stayed busy with her curtain-hanging
        business,
while you became the sad sack of your bowling team.

In a third universe, your wife wasn't an abuser.
You were both able to regard, without jealousy,
your daughter's smooth progress through
all her grades in school,

until at last she stood smiling at a graduation
with that same eager and untroubled and even cocky look
she had as a toddler.   Shortly afterwards,
you ended this marriage amicably.

There is a fourth universe to consider.   Because
had you been just a little bit bolder, or more rash,
you might have dropped out of college
to pursue a career as a writer.

Here there are two possible splinter paths.

In one, you are observed seated at a table
and the words don't come, and perhaps
there is a bottle in the vicinity, and you are in denial
about the cliché your whole life has become.

In the other, you are reading script after script
in a high-rise office and wondering if you have done
the right thing by coming to this strange place,
and hoping that you have.   Because

there is always a chance a meeting will come and you
will be able to slip your own script into the pile
under a plausible-sounding alias. And perhaps
one of those brass fasteners in the impeccably

hole-punched script will momentarily catch a glint
of LA sun, and then finally find the producer's eye.
And he will ask suddenly, apropos of nothing,
What about that one?

Ink Monkey Press is nothing without the incredible authors that fill these pages...

A.M. Burns lives in the Colorado Rockies with his partner, several dogs, cats, horses, and birds. When he's not writing, he's often fixing fences, hiking in the mountains, or flying his hawks. You can find out more about A.M. and his writing at www.amburns.com, or follow him on twitter @am_burns.

Amy Castillo lives and works in Saint Paul, Minnesota. She is a graduate of the University of Minnesota Law School and she worked in the state district courts for ten years. She loves her dog, Pete, and anything related to Star Wars. The most interesting parts of her life are unpublishable.

Anne Fox copyedits the newsletter of the California Writers Club, Berkeley Branch, as well as a community newspaper; co-copyedited the CWC Write On! story contest; and copyedits for writers of fiction and nonfiction.

Her writing has appeared in Able Muse, Tiny Lights, The Sun, and the West Winds Centennial anthology of the CWC.

Carl Palmer, president of the Tacoma Writers Club, nominee for three Pushcart Prizes and the Micro Award, from Old Mill Road in Ridgeway, VA, now lives in University Place, WA.

Catherine Gracey is an Australian writer based in Canberra. When she is not writing fiction or maintaining her blog she enjoys travelling and learning enough of foreign languages to make native speakers cringe. She has a Bachelor of Arts (Honours) in Creative Writing, and hopes that one day her friends will forget this and stop apologising for spelling errors in instant messaging conversations.

Charlotte Jones worked as a computer scientist and management consultant before finding her true love of writing and taking pictures. She has been published in more than eighty literary and commercial magazines. A photo safari in Kenya inspired this piece.

Descended from a long line of liars, **C.S. Cole** is a writer of dark fantasy, speculative fiction, and horror. Writing and automobiles are her passions and when not playing the role of gearhead in her garage, she is working on a novel about car people.

David Malone is a recent postgraduate. From Liverpool, he now works as a researcher at the BBC World Service in London. His previous works have appeared in The Momaya Annual Review, Crannog Literary Magazine, Liars' League, and Milk Money Magazine.

David Ballard's first short story was selected by Sue Grafton for publication in Best American Mystery Stories, after which he got a fat head and writer's block that lasted several years. Now that the ghosts have been cleared and all baggage stowed, he is writing again.

Gale Martin has been writing creatively since 2005, winning numerous awards for fiction. She published her first novel with Booktrope Editions in 2011. She has a master's in creative writing from Wilkes University and lives in Lancaster County, Pennsylvania.

Herika R. Raymer is a mother, wife, speculative fiction writer, and part-time editor. Her short stories can be found in a number of anthologies, to find out where visit her site at herikarraymer.webs.com.

H.L. Pauff works in marketing during the day and writes like a lunatic at night. He lives in the mountains of northeastern Pennsylvania, consumes a lot of sushi and wants to adopt a dog.

Jane White is a Special Education teacher and a life-long closet writer. The writing monkey has been on her back for 30 years, and she needs to get it off her back and onto the page where it belongs.

Jeff Moscaritolo is completing is Masters of Fine Arts at George Mason University. He enjoys writing, reading, and swing dancing. He has worked as a composition and literature instructor, and he also coaches the George Mason Forensics Team (competitive speech and debate, not cutting up dead bodies). This is what is on his mind right now, as he writes this bio: he finds passive aggressive doctors difficult to deal with. They make him reluctant to visit the doctor. Ironically, he most frequently finds their passive aggression to be aimed at the fact that he doesn't visit the doctor frequently enough. Chicken? Or egg?

Judy Klass moved to Nashville because she is a songwriter. Her short fiction has appeared in Asimov's Magazine, Bryant Literary Review, Tales of the Unanticipated, Auslander, Outer Darkness, Space & Time, Terra Incognita, Wind Magazine, The Harpur Palate, Satire and Muse & Stone, among other places. Over twenty of her one-act plays have gone up all over the country. Her full-length play CELL was nominated for an Edgar and is published by Samuel French. She teaches at Nossi College and Vanderbilt University.

Layla Layton is a writer of science fiction and contemporary fiction. She lives in Los Angeles with her husband.

Mandi M. Lynch started writing at the tender age of six, pecking away at her mother's keyboard to form her stories. Although the crayon drawings have improved, the spelling has not. Fortunately, there's spellcheck, and thanks to that, she's been published several dozen times over the last two years. She lives outside of Nashville, TN, with three cats, none of which write due to lack of thumbs.

Michele Tracy Berger is a professor, a creativity coach, a blogger and a pug-lover. She's passionate about all of these loves and plays with the order in which she avidly pursues them. Her writing has appeared in The Chapel Hill Sun, various zines, and Western North Carolina Woman.

M.V. Montgomery's poetry collection What We Did With Old Moons will be released later this year by Winter Goose Publishing.

Pamela Scott has had poetry and short fiction published in small press magazines in the UK including 'The New Writer' and 'The Dawn Treader'. She has also been published in various anthologies including 'Visible Breath', 'Crab Lines Off The Pier' and 'The Strand Book of International Poets 2011'

Robert J. Krog was born on top of a bookshelf. His father was a dictionary and his mother was a fairy tale. Robert himself was a blank journal. Upon finishing his Catholic school education and subsequent college degrees in Ancient History, he embarked on a series of adventures collecting stories to fill his pages. During that time he made a living in various ways, including teaching high school history, but generally not using his degrees. He now lives and works in Memphis, TN with his wife, Ana, a romance novel, and his children, Samantha, a puzzle book, and Sebastian, an activity book. In the pages of Robert Krog you will find many stories such as the collection, The Stone Maiden and Other Tales, and the novella, A Bag Full of Eyes. He writes as much as his obligations to a full-time job, his family, and the church allow. For more complete information, visit his website www.krogfiction.yolasite.com.

Sharon Goldberg lives in the Seattle area and previously worked as an advertising copywriter in Los Angeles, San Francisco, and Seattle. Her work has appeared or is forthcoming in Temenos, Under the Sun, The Chaffey Review, The Blotter Magazine, TheRightEyedDeer and elsewhere. Her short story "Ghost" was a finalist in the Pacific Northwest Writers Association 2011 Literary Contest. Sharon is working on a collection of short stories

Simone Martel lives in Berkeley, California, where she supports herself (sort of) editing cookbooks and self-help books. She's the author of a book of creative nonfiction, The Expectant Gardener.

Søren G. Palmer has one wife, two dogs, and four worthless liberal arts degrees.

Susan Koefod has widely published fiction, memoir and poetry. Her work has appeared in print and online literary magazines such as Turtle Quarterly, Midway Journal, Minnetonka Review, Literary Bohemian, Snakeskin, Poemeleon, The Talking Stick, No Teeth, Avocet, Prose-Poem Project, Fickle Muses and Tattoo Highway. She is at work on novel titled Albert Park: a Memoir in Lies and recently published a mystery, WASHED UP (North Star Press, 2011). A sequel, BROKEN DOWN, is scheduled for release in September 2012.

Teresa Tumminello Brader was born in New Orleans and lives in the area still, not far from a levee that is currently being strengthened. Every evening she walks the trail alongside the Pontchartrain; the estuary and its denizens are the source of much of her inspiration.

Like what you saw?

**Interested in other
Ink Monkey Press titles?**

**Want to submit
something of your own?**

Please visit us online!

http://inkmonkeymag.synthasite.com